THE BOOK OF **JUDE**

Other Books by Kimberley Heuston

The Shakeress
Dante's Daughter

THE BOOK OF
JUDE

Kimberley Heuston

FRONT STREET
Asheville, North Carolina

LIBRARY OF CONGRESS CATALOGING-IN-PUBLICATION DATA
Heuston, Kimberley Burton.
Book of Jude / Kimberley Heuston. — 1st ed.
p. cm.
Summary: In 1989, when fifteen-year-old Jude's mother wins a
Fulbright fellowship to study art in Czechoslovakia, the family
postpones a planned move to Utah to join her, but the political
situation and the move itself are too much for Jude, who is overwhelmed
by a previously undiagnosed psychological disorder.
ISBN 978-1-932425-26-0 (hardcover : alk. paper)
[1. Family life—Fiction. 2. Personality disorders—Fiction.
3. Mormons—Fiction. 4. Christian life—Fiction.
5. Communism—Fiction. 6. Moving, Household—Fiction.
7. Twins—Fiction. 8. Prague (Czech Republic)—History—
20th century—Fiction. 9. Czech Republic—History—
20th century—Fiction.] I. Title.
PZ7.H443Boo 2008   [Fic]—dc22
2007017971

FRONT STREET
An Imprint of Boyds Mills Press, Inc.
815 Church Street
Honesdale, Pennsylvania 18431

For Nathaniel
in loving memory of his magnificent mother

NEW YORK CITY

April 1989

THE **FIRST** TIME

We aren't exactly hiding. I am lying next to my twin sister, Merry, on the top shelf of the huge walk-in linen closet in the back hall of our apartment. We are just getting out of the danger zone during Mom's grumpiest hour of the day, consoling ourselves with books that have nothing to do with school and a bag of contraband tangerines.

At least, *I* am reading and eating tangerines. Merry is mostly gazing at the ceiling, which is only a few inches above our heads. I crane my neck to see the title of her thick, dusty-looking book: *Tarzan of the Apes*. No wonder. She should be reading *Ender's Game*, like me. But she read it last summer and now she won't read it again. Once she is finished with something, she moves on.

Remembering this about her irritates me. I have a cheekful of tangerine seeds, and I spit them at her.

"Knock it off, Jude," she says, without even turning her head. One of the seeds has left a smear on her glasses, and she takes them off, breathes on them, and tries to polish the smear away with the untucked tail of her shirt. Neither of us has bothered to change out of our uniform yet.

I put some more tangerine sections in my mouth and reload. The phone rings at the other end of the apartment. Someone yells something, but it's neither of our names.

That's when I get her. This time one of the seeds goes up her nose. It's rotten of me, but I can't help laughing—serious, perfect Merry with her smooth, prim ponytail and a seed hanging out of her nose.

"Sometimes you are such a jerk," she says, but I know she doesn't mean it.

We hear feet pounding along the back hallway and the closet door flies open. It's our little sister, Cory, looking like a pint-sized rodeo reject in jeans, denim shirt, and cowboy boots.

"Mom says everyone at the elevator right now!" Cory orders. Cory is eight, seven years younger than we are, and likes it when she can be in charge.

Without thinking, Merry starts to sit up and cracks her head hard on the ceiling.

I wince in sympathy.

"Ouch!" she says, and rubs her head. "Is everything okay?"

"As far as I know," Cory says. "Mom just said to get a move on."

"Heads up," I say. I throw my paperback over Merry's shoulder into the corner of the shelf, then roll over so that I hang by my hands and drop to the floor like a cat.

Merry mutters, "Show-off." She follows more slowly,

feeling for each shelf with her foot as she lowers herself to the floor. When she's halfway there, we hear Mom coming.

We have the drill down. Merry climbs back up to get rid of the evidence while I run interference.

"Hi, Mom," I say, emerging into the hall and casually closing the closet door behind me.

Mom, who has clearly been concentrating on something else, tucks her short, thick chestnut hair behind one ear and focuses on me.

"You girls don't have food out of the kitchen, do you?" she says after a minute.

"Of course not," I say, pleased to hear that I have gotten the note of injured innocence exactly right.

Mom leans forward and picks something off my cheek. It's a bit of white tangerine membrane. Oops.

Merry emerges from the closet, her hand still in the pocket of her skirt where she has no doubt stashed the peels. She gives an unconvincing start of surprise. "Oh, hi, Mom."

"You two are totally busted," Mom says. "But there's no time for that now. Your father just called to say he wants to meet us at the coffee shop."

We *never* go out to eat. Never. Not even to McDonald's. Dad's in education, Mom's a graduate student in art history at NYU, and there are three of us kids. Do the math. We may live on Park Avenue, but that's only because the apartment comes with the job. Day to day, we're broke.

"What's up?"

Mom's lake-blue eyes turn opaque. "Dad must want to eat out," she says, brushing by me to get to her study at the back of the apartment. Automatically I breathe in so I can smell her perfume. "I'll just get my pocketbook," she calls over her shoulder. "Meet you guys at the elevator."

"So do you have any idea of what's up?" I ask Cory as we follow her down the hall.

Cory hitches her jeans up around her narrow hips, the better to show off her cowboy boots. "Dad called and we're meeting him for dinner."

"Yeah, we know," Merry says. "Mom said. But do you know *why* he wants to meet us for dinner?"

Cory looks at us as though we're stupid. "It's dinnertime."

It's a soft blue evening, wet and smelling of spring, even in the city. When we get to the restaurant, Dad's waiting under the awning with a goofy smile on his face and a bouquet of blood-red roses. When he catches sight of Mom, his face lights up and he throws his arms around her and gives her a big, smacking kiss.

"Eeww!" Cory cries, and covers her eyes.

Merry and I look at each other. Something is definitely up. But what? Can't be school. Mom doesn't defend her dissertation for another month. The last time Dad did something like this was when Cory ...

Memories of a small bundle of pink flannel spread through me like a warm summer wave. "Mom's having a baby," I mouth to Merry over Cory's head. I can't stop a foolish grin from spreading across my face. Mom and Dad have been saying that we're moving so they can both teach at BYU, but that's not the real reason. The real reason is that we need more room for the baby.

I remember the smell of Cory, and the feel of her soft pink cheek against my lips. Anticipation fizzes through my veins like iced champagne. "Isn't it *great*?"

But Merry isn't smiling back. Her eyes, squinting slightly behind her glasses, are on our parents. She looks like a scientist examining a specimen. "I don't think so."

I am flabbergasted. Merry is the world's biggest guppy about babies. Much worse than I am. "You don't think it's great?"

Merry shoots a glance at Cory and sidles over next to me. "I don't think Mom's pregnant," she says, so close to my ear that it tickles.

"Of course she is," I say, rubbing at my ear. "Dad brought her *flowers*. He never brings her flowers. What else could it be?"

Merry shrugs. "I don't know," she says. "Just not a baby. She's not in that place anymore."

She says the words like they are no big deal. But they are. They're a huge deal.

"How can you say that?" I demand. "What other place would she be? She's our *mother*. It's what she *does*."

"Bet you five bucks," she says.

"That it's not a baby?"

She nods.

"Make it ten."

"You're on," she says.

* * *

"What happened at school today?" Dad wants to know once we're inside and settled and the waiter has taken our order.

Cory tells him about coming up with testable hypotheses to explain the relationship between April showers and May flowers. Dad listens intently, bending toward her with one arm crooked protectively across the back of the red vinyl banquette they share. His other hand is on Mom's knee. His blue eyes, paler than hers, are tired behind his wire-rimmed glasses, and he is getting little lines at the corner of his mouth and eyes. But he looks like Dad, happy to be with us. Of course it's a baby.

Cory finally shuts up, and I swallow a mouthful of corned beef and sauerkraut. "So, Dad, what's up?"

Dad clears his throat. "Well, there *is* something your mother and I want to talk to you about."

Here it comes.

"Ginny?" he says.

Mom takes a big breath and stretches her hands out on the table in front of her. "You girls know that I've been studying Alfons Mucha."

Alfons Mucha was a Czech painter who went to Paris at the turn of the twentieth century and became a famous illustrator. "Yeah? So?" I prod.

"I applied for a fellowship, and I won it," she says. There's a little pause, and you can see that she doesn't want to miss how sweet the words she's about to say are going to taste in her mouth. "I won a Fulbright."

Four words. Four little words. They aren't anything, just a puff of air. But they smash into me with the deep, dull thud of a hockey puck hurled right at my diaphragm. I have no idea what she's talking about, but I know that whatever it is is going to change everything. And there's not going to be a baby.

Merry gives an excited little yelp and leans across me to hug Mom, almost knocking over my Coke. "That's wonderful! Congratulations! Why didn't you tell us you had applied?"

"We didn't want you guys to worry about it until we knew for sure," Mom says, her cheeks pink and her eyes bright. She looks young and pretty and a little shy and not like a mother at all.

"Worry about what?" Cory says, looking tense. "Is it something bad?"

Mom laughs. "No, honey, it's something very, very good. They're giving me money so I can spend a year studying in Czechoslovakia."

Czechoslovakia?

"Not Paris?" Merry says, looking disappointed.

"Paris, shmaris," Dad says. "Anyone can go to Paris. But Czechoslovakia—do you guys have any idea what a huge honor it is for your mom to be invited to study there?"

"Is it a school?" Cory wants to know. "Like when you got into NYU?"

Mom smiles at her. "No, bugs. Czechoslovakia is a country. A beautiful country right next to Germany and Austria."

"Like in *The Sound of Music*," Merry says. That's her favorite movie. Don't ask me why.

Cory looks worried. "*The Sound of Music*? What about the Gestapo?"

"You don't have to worry about them," Dad says, patting her hand. "They're long gone."

"Yeah, the Communists are a big improvement," I say, sort of under my breath, but loud enough so that I know Cory will hear.

"Communists?" Cory says.

"Czechoslovakia's behind the Iron Curtain," I tell her. "Where all the Communists live. You know. Like Boris and Natasha."

Cory loves Bullwinkle cartoons and is especially fond of Bullwinkle's sidekick, Rocky the Squirrel. When we first moved to New York, she had a lot of nightmares, and my parents bought her a little stuffed Rocky to guard her pillow. It worked for a long time, until she saw a short guy on the subway with a pencil mustache wearing a black trench coat and a black hat and convinced herself that he was Boris, Rocky's nemesis. She made Mom mail Rocky to our Utah grandparents that very day to keep him safe.

"Congratulations, Mom," I say, talking loud and fast so no one can stop me. "It's really great you won and all. Too bad you have to turn it down."

"Turn it down?" she says sharply. "Why would I turn it down?"

"What about Boris and Natasha?" Cory says, her eyes stretched really big so that she won't cry.

"Jude was just teasing you, honey," Dad says in his head-master voice. "Weren't you, Jude?"

I shrug. "I guess," I mumble into what's left of my sandwich. I shove it away. I straighten up as something else occurs to me. "What about BYU? I thought you signed a contract."

"We told them when we interviewed that I had applied for a Fulbright, and they said that if I won they'd hold my place for a year."

"So you're going to Czechoslovakia instead of Provo?"

"Yes, sweetheart," she says, a little impatiently. "That's what we're trying to tell you."

These words aren't stones. They are clear, like jellyfish, and as they pass in front of my eyes they change the shape of things.

Everyone always talks about how "centered" my mother is, how okay she is with herself. But centered can be dangerous. You can't argue with centered.

I can't breathe. There are strange ripples in my chest now, and I can't get enough air.

"Why are you *doing* this?" I say.

"Judith Grace," Dad says sharply. "What has gotten into you?"

What has gotten into *me*? What has gotten into *them*? "I'm trying to understand why it doesn't seem to be bothering anyone but me that your wife and our mother is being so *selfish*."

There is a short silence, and then everyone starts talking at once.

Dad puts up his hands until everyone shuts up. "Jude, that is a grossly unfair accusation," he says. "Your mother and I have prayed long and hard about this, and we would not have made this decision unless we believed that it was the best thing not only for her, but for all of us."

I start to interrupt, and his hand goes up again.

"Look, kids, this is something we've spent a lot of time thinking and praying and fasting about. We wouldn't be taking you if we thought you would be in any danger."

I pounce on his words. "Say that again?"

"I said that your mother and I would never knowingly put any of you in danger."

"Not that part," I say. "The other thing. You're taking us with you? We're all going?"

"Of course we are," Mom says, and it's the voice she uses when one of us wakes up from a nightmare.

I have to make sure. "All of us?" I say. "Dad and Merry and me and Cory? For the whole time? Not just a visit?"

"Of course," she says again. "What else would you do?"

Of course, she says. Of *course* we're going. What else would we do?

The strangeness that has been shimmering between me and everyone else thins to a wisp and blows away. I feel the world hiccup as everything settles back where it belongs, and I give a hiccup too, a kind of laugh, as my lungs remember how to do their job.

"So how is this going to work?" Merry asks. "What's Dad going to do?"

"We've actually had the most amazing piece of luck," Dad says. "There's an international school in Prague, and the head has had some health problems this year. They needed a last-minute replacement, and they offered me the job. So it looks like you girls haven't gotten rid of me yet."

"We'll be at this international school?" Merry asks.

"Yep."

"And it's coed?"

Dad laughs. "Yes. It *is* coed. Not very big—about eighty kids. But coed."

"So we're not going to Utah," Cory says.

"We are, just a year later than we planned."

I close my eyes, and when I open them again Mom is washing some ketchup off Cory's face and Dad is stealing a bite of Merry's pie and everything is normal. Everything is completely normal.

I made a big deal out of nothing. It was my mistake. Mine. I'm such an idiot sometimes. I bite down hard on the inside of my cheek to show myself that I understand that I made a mistake.

BLADES

I wander through that night and the next morning wrapped in a noise-absorbing bubble. Everyone is talk-talk-talking about Czechoslovakia, and how exciting it will be to get to know a new place together, and how our dog, Toby, will really be happier spending the year at the vineyard with Nana and Grandpop than having to go into doggy quarantine for months before she's allowed into Czechoslovakia, and I just want them all to shut up. We've spent the whole year talk-talk-talking about Utah, and I can't switch gears this quickly. So I smile and nod, but mostly I'm doing things like memorizing the exact line of the shades flapping on our bedroom window and not thinking, *not thinking,* about the strange clear jelly that has come back, spreading itself between me and everyone else.

School is a huge relief. The morning is one long round of tests and in-class essays and announcements, and there's no time to talk about things that are changing too fast. At lunch I beat a hasty retreat to the dining room with my friend Lexy before Merry can say anything. But as I play with the meatloaf and green beans on my plate and watch Lexy wolf down her Tofu Surprise, my own mouth betrays me.

"So Mom won a Fulbright," I hear myself saying. "We're going to Czechoslovakia for a year before the trek west."

Lexy puts down her vegan hideousness and looks delighted. "That's ab fab," she says. "Way to go, Mrs. W!"

I poke at the dish of apple pie, but that doesn't look any better. I push my tray away.

"Hey, do they know about the water balloons?" she asks. Four years ago, as a gesture of solidarity with the Russian dissident Sakharov, who was on a hunger strike, we two fifth graders threw water balloons out of the eighth-floor art room window at the Russian Embassy across the street. The Russians were not amused. Neither was my father.

There's a thought. I feel a little better. "Do you think it's enough to keep us out?"

Lexy stares at me, her bright mouse eyes narrowing. "Judith Grace Wheelock. Please tell me you made a big, noisy fuss over your mother. A Fulbright's a really big deal. Tell me you didn't get all selfish and whiny."

I use my fork to arrange the leftover peas on my plate into a perfect circle.

"You don't deserve her," Lexy says, shaking her head and reaching for her orange. "You really don't."

"I know," I say, although I don't know, not really. I look around. No one can hear us. My heart is thumping so hard that I don't realize what I'm going to say until I've said it. "Lex, can I ask you something?"

"Shoot."

"Last night, when they told us. At first I thought Mom meant that she was going to Czechoslovakia for a year without us. It made everything—different."

Lexy looks at me while the half-peeled orange waits in her hands.

"Yeah, so, it made things different," she prompts.

"It made them strange," I say. "Really awful and scary and bad."

"Yeah?" she says.

"Do you think it's weird that I thought she meant she was leaving for a year?"

Lexy breaks her orange in two and peels off a section. She waves it around in the air for a minute, thinking. "Well, it's maybe a little weird," she says. "Going off by herself isn't something I'd expect your mother to do. But it's certainly in the realm of possibility. What does everyone else think about Czechoslovakia?"

I shrug. "They're mostly okay with it. My dad is going to run the international school there, and Merry's all excited because it's coed." I hesitate. "Cory's a little freaked out."

"In a generalized, Cory sort of way? Or about something specific?"

Because of me. Because I was mad, and I didn't think, and I said something that I knew would scare her. I open my mouth, then close it.

The bell rings and I stand up fast and take my tray over to the dish station. Lexy is right behind me. "Your poor mother," she's saying. "The achievement of a lifetime and all you guys can do is moan about how Julie Andrews would never do that to the Von Trapp children."

I feel slapped. I want Lexy to shut up. I want everyone to shut up and just leave me alone. Too much is happening, and I can't stay on top of it all.

I scrape my leftovers into the garbage with such force that half of them land on the floor. Shirley, the lunch lady, doesn't say anything, just hands me a rag. I get down on the floor and clean up the mess. I am furious, but I'm not sure whether it's at Shirley or Lexy or Mom or maybe even Cory.

Lexy doesn't say anything, just waits for me. But as we clatter down the back stairs to our lockers on the third floor, I know she is thinking about what a loser I am, how I don't deserve a mother like mine.

The more I think about it, the madder I get. If Mom would just be a mom, none of this would be happening. We wouldn't have to go to Czechoslovakia. We wouldn't even have to leave New York. The only reason we're leaving is that she wants to teach instead of staying home with us the way she's supposed to.

It takes me three tries to get the stupid combination on my locker to work, and then I have to root around in the garbage piled up in the bottom for my physics notebook.

Lexy slams her locker shut. "Jude," she says, "come on. We're going to be late."

I look at her. Some of the strangeness from last night is back. It's in my mouth—an odd metallic taste.

"Are you all right?" she says. "Jude? We've got to go."

I look around and see that the hall is clearing as people go to class. "I'm fine," I say. "I was just thinking about what you said about Mom not being Julie Andrews."

"Think about it later, okay?" she says.

The bell rings and she swears.

I still haven't found my notebook, but Merry will let me copy her notes. I grab some random papers so I'll have something to write on and slam my locker shut.

By the time we get up to the fifth floor and in the door of the physics room, Dr. Palmer is halfway through explaining the lab. Merry is sitting on one of the high stools near the front of the room, taking neat, rapid notes. I walk by and jiggle Merry's elbow accidentally on purpose; she hates to make mistakes, especially when she's writing in pen. Without taking her eyes from Dr. Palmer, she sticks out her leg so that I trip over it.

Dr. Palmer stops talking.

I sit down as fast as I can and begin to smooth out the papers in my hand so I can take notes.

She still isn't talking. I smooth the papers some more and write the date at the top.

"Miss Wheelock," she says in her throaty cigarette voice.

"Yes, Dr. Palmer," I say, looking at her reluctantly. Her arms are folded and her lips are tight. This is not a good sign.

"This is fifth period," she says.

"Yes, I know," I say.

"That means you are coming from lunch," she continues.

"Yes."

"You were late to my class from *lunch*?" she says, giving the last word a little bit of extra zing.

I feel myself beginning to flush. I like Dr. Palmer. She's fair, and she knows her stuff.

"Yes, I was," I admit.

Dr. Palmer makes an impatient little click against her teeth. She is a tall, lean woman who wears her smooth blond hair parted on the side, like Rose Marie on *The Dick Van Dyke Show*, but without the little black velvet bow.

"When you choose to be late," she says, "you are also choosing to interrupt the learning process of your classmates."

"I'm sorry," I say, and I mean it.

She sighs. "Consider this fair warning," she says. "Next time it will be Friday Study."

Our school gets out at lunch on Fridays so that all the rich kids can beat the traffic to their country houses. Staying for what amounts to detention on a Friday afternoon stinks.

"I'm really sorry," I say again.

She shakes her head a little, her lips still tight, then goes back to discussing the lab. I try to take notes, but I can't concentrate.

With a screech everyone pushes their lab stools back. I hop down a little late and go stand with Merry, who will show me what to do.

Dr. Palmer has set up the wave tank on the cabinet at the side of the room, but there's no water in it, just a bunch of tiny bright blue silicon beads.

"Okay, girls, who did their reading? What's the lab on today?"

Merry and Lexy both start waving their hands in the air.

"Lexy?"

"The principle of inertia," Lexy says.

"Good," says Dr. Palmer. "And what exactly is the principle of inertia? Class?"

"Objects at rest remain at rest and objects in motion remain in motion until worked upon by an opposing force," we dutifully recite.

"That's right," Dr. Palmer says, picking up a pile of books and carrying them over to where Muffin is sitting, totally zoned out. "Objects in motion remain in motion and objects at rest remain at rest, until moved upon"—she drops the books with a thud, and Muffin jumps about a mile in the air—"by an outside force." Everyone laughs.

"So we've seen the object at rest," Dr. Palmer continues. "Can anyone think of an everyday example of something remaining in motion?"

"No," says Lexy. "It doesn't exist in our world. Skiers and skaters try, but friction and gravity always slow them down."

"That's right," Dr. Palmer says. "Like this." She picks up a ball made out of some kind of heavy metal and sets it rolling at me across the top of the lab bench. "Think fast!" she says.

I drop my pen and try to get my hands in position to catch the ball, but I needn't have worried. The ball is so heavy that it slows to a stop before it gets anywhere close to the edge.

"Now let's try it here," she says. She picks up the ball and sets it rolling in the tank of little blue beads. And it's amazing. It just keeps going. When it gets to the side, it ricochets and keeps right on going for at least a full minute before it finally eases to a stop.

"So the procedure for the lab ..." Dr. Palmer starts to explain, but I stop listening. I reach into the tank and set the ball going again, and imagine what it would be like to be that ball, passed along by a million zillion little hands. Never stopping, just zooming through the galaxy. Never worrying about what happens when you get to the end, because there is no end. Just going and going and going.

Last period Tuesday is a PE and arts block that goes until five o'clock. This term all three of us—me and Lexy and Merry— are signed up for softball at the park on East End. I go to my locker, dig out my sweat pants and pull them on underneath my skirt, exchange my Topsiders for my Adidas, and stuff the shoes and skirt into my backpack. Ready. I look around. Merry is sitting on a bench tying her sneakers. "Lexy says go on, she'll catch up," she says. "You ready?"

The nice thing about Merry is that she doesn't carry a grudge. Either that, or she figures getting me in trouble with Dr. Palmer makes us even.

I sling on my backpack and Merry grabs her big embroidered cotton thing and we're off.

We burst out of the school and it's a perfect day, the first one of the year. It's much too nice a day to walk, and soon the two of us are jogging along. I jump up to touch the traffic lights we pass. Energy sparks out the bottom of my fingers and the soles of my feet, and when I have to wait for Merry to catch up at the corners I feel like I might explode if I can't start moving again.

We're the first ones at the park. We pull our gloves out of

our bags, but neither one of us brought a ball, so we have to stand around until the others get here.

"Here comes Lexy," Merry finally says. I glance back over my shoulder, but the sidewalk is empty.

"Where?"

"There," she says, pointing at the street.

It takes my brain a minute to understand what my eyes are seeing. Lexy's brown head, as round and neat as an otter's, is bobbing through traffic. She's not running. It looks like she's skiing. But she can't be skiing. There's no snow. The light changes, the cars pass, and I understand. She's wearing ski boots, but they are not attached to skis. They're roller skates, but not like any roller skates I've ever seen.

"Hey," Lexy says as she draws up next to us, her freckled face flushed with effort but her mouth split in a wide grin.

"Hey," I say. I can't keep my eyes off her roller skates. I've never seen anything like them before—purple plastic with bright green laces. The wheels are different, too. They're plastic, not metal, and they line up in one column instead of two by two. "What are those?"

"Rollerblades," she says.

"They're outrageous," Merry says.

"Can I try?" I ask.

Lexy hesitates.

"Pleeeeese," I plead.

"Oh, all right," Lexy says. She squats down, and almost before she has them untied I am tugging them off her feet. She shows me how to stop, and then I push off.

The pavement here by the park is cracked and uneven,

and the rollerblades are harder to control than regular roller skates, especially because Lexy's feet are longer than mine and my ankles are wobbling all over the place. But by the time I've gone a block I've got the rhythm in my feet, hips, and shoulders. There's a ramp for wheelchairs at the corner, and I leave the sidewalk for the smoother surface of the asphalt. The light changes and cars breathe hot exhaust at me, but I don't care. The rollerblades are unbelievable. I am riding a wave. Faster and faster, until my feet fall behind the rest of me. I know it will hurt, but at the moment that I leave the ground, I don't care. I am flying.

BLESSING

I'm holding a baby who loves me. We are swooping through woods and vines toward the clear blue sky so fast and true that nothing can stop us. *This* is the feeling I remember, the feeling I've been looking for—the power of knowing and being known. Of receiving and being received.

Remember!

It's in his bright eyes and the sweet roundness of his mouth.

Remember!

The word dances in my blood ...

Remember!

... music pulsing through the marrow of my bones. I brush my lips against the peach down of his cheek, inhaling until every cell of my body is bathed in light and love.

We are knit together, we two.

The violence of our parting flays the skin from my body, shredding muscle and splintering bone. But the worst is that my shattered vessel can no longer hold the rhythm and order of that lovely deep music. I feel it leave me, leaking away, drop by drop, until all that is left is emptiness that jerks, hardens, and blazes into pain.

I open my eyes. I am lying in the street, my cheek held fast by the grit of asphalt, support for which I am grateful. Lexy is there, and Merry, but no order, no sense.

Sirens. Jostling. Pain like a knife at my heart.

I see myself reflected in my father's glasses, a small, broken insect.

"Jude," he says, speaking slowly. "You're at Lenox Hill Hospital. There was an accident. You bumped your head pretty hard and probably broke your collarbone."

I fumble for words, but they are hard to find. "Oh," I finally manage.

"They're coming to take you to x-ray in a minute, but I'd like to give you a blessing first, okay?"

"Okay," I say. Something really bad slams against my chest. Something I might have done. "What happened to Lexy's blades? Did I hurt them? Are they ruined?"

"They're fine, sweetie. Not a scratch on them. Stay still, now."

Tears are leaking out of my eyes, like the music, and what's stupid is that I can't raise my arm to wipe them away. "I'm sorry, Dad. I'm so sorry."

"Hey," he says, going for the handkerchief he keeps in his pocket. "None of that, now." He shakes it out and kind of blots at my face, trying to help, but he's afraid to press too hard and it feels like he's mostly smearing stuff around.

"Thanks, Dad. I'm good," I say.

"Sure?" he says.

"Yeah."

He folds up the handkerchief and clears his throat. "You ready?"

"Ready."

He pokes his head into the hall to make sure no one's coming, then closes the door. I feel the familiar weight of his hands settling on my head, and I go still, trying to make a space for the Spirit to nestle around my heart. But I can't. There is no quiet space in me.

"Judith Grace Wheelock," Dad says. "In the name of Jesus Christ and by the authority of the holy Melchizedek priesthood which I bear, I have the privilege of giving you a father's blessing of healing and comfort at the beginning of what will be an eventful and important year in your life's journey."

That's not right. That's not the way it's supposed to go at all. It's supposed to start with how my Heavenly Father loves me and how proud He is of the person I'm trying to become, and then say something about making me better, and then we're done.

"Judith, I would remind you that you are named for your great-great-grandmother, a pioneer who crossed the plains with little besides her children and her faith. Her life was not an easy one. She buried five of those she loved—leaving first her mother, then her husband, then her sons and her baby daughter in foreign ground she would not see again. Yet she and one daughter, your great-grandmother, survived the journey, and left a legacy of faith and strength that have shaped the lives of generations.

"Your Heavenly Father reminds you that this is your heritage. Like your great-great-grandmother, you, too, are called to be a pioneer. Your forebears walked paths that, while strange and unfamiliar, could be named and measured. You will not have that comfort on your journey. You will have no map, you will have no plan, indeed at times you will have no language to describe the nature of your journey and the challenges that face you. Be comforted, Judith, in the knowledge that your Heavenly Father and your brother Jesus Christ will attend you. Put your hand in theirs, and they will lead you, in due course, to safety, to warm hands and loving hearts, to peace.

"I give you promise, Judith, that as you look back upon your life's journey, you will see that your footprints have been lamps to the feet of those that follow. You will be to them as a Savior on Mount Zion.

"Your Heavenly Father counsels you, Judith, to ponder these promises, to let them work in your heart and your soul. He counsels you to discipline yourself, to the extent that you are able, to be wise and cautious in your choices, to consider carefully the consequences, both now and in the eternities, of your thoughts and actions. He gives you promise, Judith, that as you do this, he will put his arms around you and lead you in paths of righteousness and peace. You will be numbered among the Pure in Heart, and you will see God.

"I seal this blessing on your head, with the assurance that you are a choice and precious daughter of your Heavenly Father, and that He is eager for you to complete your life's mission and return to Him, and that the injuries you received today will heal with no more than the normal amount of discomfort and inconvenience. And I do so in the name of Jesus Christ, amen."

His hands drop from my head.

"Well," Dad says.

I can't think of anything to say.

"Well," he says again.

Apparently he can't think of anything to say, either.

The silence grows awkward. "I wasn't expecting *that*," Dad finally admits. He scrubs at his hair so that it stands up at the back of his head like a little boy's. "Sounds like it might be a ..." He searches for the word. "An interesting year for you, sweetheart." He fumbles with the sidebars of my bed, trying to lower them so he can come sit next to me, but before he figures out how they work, the door opens. An attendant in scrubs and dreadlocks shambles in, holding a chart.

"You Wheelock?" he asks, but the question is apparently rhetorical. He hangs the chart on my bed and pushes some kind of release. The ceiling swivels around him, and that's it. We're gone.

Goodbye to all that, I tell the dirty rectangles of fluorescent ceiling fixtures swooping above my aching head, and close my eyes.

CHURCH

I did indeed break my collarbone. I also scored a nice concussion that gets me excused from three tests and a paper. The first few days are not pleasant, but by Sunday I'm pretty much back to normal. As a bonus, my shoulder and chest are turning this completely sick green, which grosses everyone out. Besides, it's Fast Sunday, the first Sunday of the month, and Mom says I don't have to fast because I'm on painkillers.

I like the painkillers. They are like a little echo of that effortless, no-friction, flying way of being.

I explain this to Mom in her room while she is putting on her pantyhose. The bathroom door opens behind her and I get a whiff of soap and Dad's aftershave as he comes out in his church clothes, whistling a stupid John Denver song.

"Whit," Mom says, "I think maybe Jude should stay home."

"Does your shoulder hurt, honey?" Dad asks.

"Nope. I'm snug as a bug in a rug," I tell him.

"She's flying," Mom says, doing some eyebrow action.

"I certainly am," I agree.

Dad turns his attention to his tie. "She'll be fine. If it gets too bad, one of us can always bring her home."

"By 'one of us,' I assume you mean you?" Mom says.

"Naturally," he says. "Five bucks if you get me out of Priesthood, Jude."

"Whit!" Mom says sharply. "That's not funny. He's just teasing you, sweetheart."

But behind her, Dad holds up one hand spread wide and points to it with the other, mouthing, "Five bucks."

The sisters are all lying in wait for us when we get off the elevator at church. Apparently the word has gotten out about Czechoslovakia, because they don't waste any time oohing and ahhing over my sling.

Julie Brinton, a young mother from Provo who sews matching outfits for her three little girls, is first off the block. "Sister Wheelock, what's this I hear about you winning some big academic honor?" she trills, her eyes steely below her flawlessly applied eye shadow. "Congratulations! How *do* you do it all without neglecting your family?"

Her husband is trying to make partner at one of the big law firms downtown, but if you ask me, she's the one with the killer instinct.

"With grace and efficiency," says Sister Morgan, the bishop's wife, giving Mom a big hug. "Congratulations, Ginny. What an adventure you'll have! And good gracious, Jude, what happened to you?"

"Roller skating," I say. I like Sister Morgan a lot. "No big deal. It'll mend."

"How do you girls feel about the move?"

"We're going behind the Metal Curtain," Cory says.

"The *Iron* Curtain," Mom corrects her.

"Oh, people are people wherever they live," says Sister Morgan.

"I've always wanted to live in Prague," Hester Lynn says. Hester is a very sophisticated-looking model from Idaho. She's been on all the big covers—*Vogue, Cosmopolitan*—and they used her as the model for the mannequins at Barney's. "That's where they filmed *Amadeus,* you know. All the beautiful clothes. All the wonderful parties."

"That was a *movie*," Winnie Reardon sniffs. Sister Reardon is a single mother from Harlem and thinks the rest of us lead sheltered lives, which is true, and that it is her job to tell it like it is.

But before she can, Chrissy Reynolds darts out of the crowd, squealing with delight. Chrissy, who is two years old, prefers not to wear clothing. In fact, she's not wearing anything right now but her underpants. Her mother is probably busy setting up chairs for the little kids in Primary.

"Hey, girlfriend!" I say. "What's shaking? No, I can't pick you up today. I've got an owie."

"Why do you have that thing on your arm?" Chrissy says, trying to tug it off.

I tense my shoulder. "No, don't," I gasp. "I have an owie. Leave it alone."

"Christina Louise Reynolds!"

Chrissy giggles and scrambles behind me, her curved little stomach rigid with excitement.

Her mother appears in the hall, holding Chrissy's discarded shoes, tights, and dress.

Sister Reynolds sees Mom, and her eyes well up. "Oh, Ginny, what will we do without you?" she says, and gives Mom a big hug. "I'm sorry," she apologizes, dabbing at her mascara a little too late. "Fasting always makes me so emotional."

Fortunately, Brother Christenson starts playing the organ prelude in the chapel before everyone has a complete meltdown. This is the signal that it's time to stop chatting and find seats. We all shuffle in, getting a program from Brother Ehrlich at the door and then spreading out across the benches.

I zone out a little during the familiar pattern of hymn, prayer, announcements. It's pleasant here in the sun. During the sacrament hymn Dad stretches his arm along the back of the bench and I snuggle in against his scratchy tweed jacket, breathing in his aftershave. He moves his finger along the hymnal, helping Cory keep track of the words. He sings a little off-key. Chrissy's brother Mike, who is a year younger than we are and has a crush on Merry, blushes like he always does when he gets to our row with the tray of bread and, a few minutes later, the one with water.

You can tell when the sacrament ends by the rustle of mothers distributing paper, pencils, and plastic tubs of Cheerios to their offspring. Brother Gledhill is first to the podium, as always. I like Brother Gledhill, mostly because he's one of the few regulars who do not mistake length of drone for depth of spiritual commitment. Sixty seconds and boom, he's done.

No one follows him for a while, long enough for me to worry that some misguided soul will decide this is a golden opportunity to teach little Nephi or little Zoe the joys of bearing testimony. I'm sure those performances are meaningful to their parents. But for everyone else?

I look around the congregation, willing someone, *anyone*, who has reached puberty to stand up. As if he has heard me, Brother Ehrlich, the little old German man who gives out the programs, struggles to his feet. Slowly, painfully, he makes his way up to the stand. You can tell he has shrunk. His jacket hangs from shoulders that look like they belong on a bigger man, and his pants are belted up around his armpits, showing two inches of white socks above his thick-soled black shoes. As he passes our bench, I see white old-man whiskers. He hasn't shaved, and his tie is crooked.

Merry bends forward to catch Mom's eye. "He looks terrible," she whispers. "What happened?"

"Sister Ehrlich has been quite ill," Mom whispers back.

I look back at his seat, and sure enough, no Sister Ehrlich with her lumpy old-lady shoes.

"Bruddas and sisters," Brother Ehrlich begins in his thick German accent. "This morning at about four o'clock, my beautiful Ruth passed away." The room gets very quiet as he begins to cry. He waits for a minute until he can go on. "She was a good woman," he says, and stops again. "She has not left me yet, and for that I am very grateful," he almost whispers.

He stands up a little straighter. "Bruddas and sisters, I hope you will not think ill of me, but these last few hours have been very sweet. Things were hard in Germany after the war, and we lost our little boy, our little Freddie. There has been a hole in her heart ever since, and I think to rejoice today that that hole is filled. That she and Freddie are finally together again. You know, she was not a beautiful woman. Even when we were younger, she was never a beautiful woman. But she was beautiful *here*." He strikes his chest. "She was beautiful *here*," he repeats. "And I am grateful that the Lord gave me such a partner. I hope it will not be too long until we are together again, the three of us. But today, today my Ruth is with her Savior. She is telling him the beautiful story of her life. And today there is no more grief, no more disappointment. Today she is healed and joyful, and she is with people who see her as I see her, who love her as I love her." He stops again, takes a handkerchief from his pocket, and carefully blows his nose.

"You have been our family," he says. "Ever since we have come to this country, you have been our family. I am grateful that I have had a calling to greet each of you every Sunday. We have watched you grow up and worried about you and celebrated your babies and your successes." He wags his finger at us. "You did not know, maybe, that you were our children, but we knew. We knew. And you made my Ruth a happy momma. I thank you for her, and I thank God for her, and for the gospel that teaches two old Germans like us to live lives that will bring us back to our Savior. And I say these things in the name of Jesus Christ, amen."

"Amen," we all say. Everyone is crying now, even the bishop, because right now we are all part of the same story, and none of it is strange or bad.

THE **END**

Chalk squeaks, and I jump. It's just Dr. Palmer, writing the time on the board. 9:30. The exam is half over. One more hour. One more hour until Thatcher is done.

I look down at my bluebook. Last term I had the class high. Last term I had so much extra time that I answered the last essay question in a code I invented on the spot, a code that I know Dr. Palmer broke because she used it to write my progress report. But there is no code today—at least, not one I can understand. I've written down some random formulas, but I don't think I've actually answered any of the questions. I pick up the exam and give it a good hard look. But I can't get it in focus.

I lean forward and put my forehead against the cool black stone of the lab table until my eyes decide to work. I squint at the exam paper sideways, my cheek still resting on the table. The exam is actually quite beautiful, with elegantly shaped symbols on crisp white paper.

"Five minutes," Dr. Palmer says. My stomach lurches. Five

minutes. I have to solve some problems. But I can't. Time keeps starting and stopping.

I look over at Merry at the next table. She looks different in civilian clothes, which we're allowed to wear during exams. The T-shirt and short jean skirt she's wearing showing off her figure as clearly as her strappy leather sandals show off the shape of her feet, and her hair is tucked back into a smooth French braid. I look down at my feet, at the thick athletic socks stuffed not very comfortably into my untied Adidas. I stare at them for a while. I know those sneakers. I have drawn on their white rubber tread with my blue ballpoint pen. I move one foot, and the sneaker moves, too. Those must be my feet.

"Okay, girls, put your pencils down and pass your bluebooks to the right," Dr. Palmer says. I watch a hand put down a pencil and close the bluebook in front of me. I close my eyes tightly and then open them. The hand is mine again.

"Yo, Jude. Anytime this century."

I look up and Lexy is holding out her hand for my exam. I slip the questions inside the bluebook and hand it to her.

Now it's done.

"Have a wonderful summer, girls," Dr. Palmer says, taking the exams from Lexy.

And that's all. I feel like there should be more. A ceremony. A ritual. Something to say that Merry and I are leaving and things will be different now. But even as I think it, Dr. Palmer walks out of the room, followed by Merry and her friend Lilibet and then everyone else. Within a minute, the room is empty, except for me and Lexy. And soon Lexy will be gone, too. She is leaving tomorrow to spend a month in Africa with her father, who is shooting a documentary on endangered animals of the Serengeti.

A wave of tenderness washes over me as I think of Lexy in Africa, a gangly, bright-eyed mouse alone on the savannah. It occurs to me that I have no idea how to say goodbye to her. I should have asked Merry. She would have known what to do. But I didn't think. I didn't plan. The moving men are coming today and I promised Mom I'd come right home to pack. Now there's no time to find any kind of gift—even just words—to offer my friend.

"So are you coming or what?" Lexy asks.

"Coming where?"

"Sandwiches from the deli. My treat."

My stomach sinks. "I'm so sorry, Lexy," I say. "But I promised ..."

"I checked it with your mom," Lexy says. "She said go, have a good time, and she'll see you tonight."

"She did?"

Lexy is beaming so hard that her chin, which is not that noticeable to begin with, has completely disappeared. With her straight, colorless hair shoved behind her big, stick-out ears she looks more like a mouse than ever, but a mouse with a light turned on inside. It's all I can do not to burst into tears. I didn't see this goodbye coming, but Lexy did.

"Well, cool," I manage after a minute. "What are we waiting for?"

Lexy buys us ham sandwiches with mayo at the Greek deli around the corner—the great big thick ones on Kaiser rolls that my family can never afford—and brownies at Greenberg's. But then, instead of turning west toward the park, Lexy heads east toward the subway.

"Just one quick stop," she says when I protest. "It won't take long, I promise."

We get off at Fourteenth Street and head to Paragon Sports. It turns out that Lexy has brought me here to buy me rollerblades, so that I can get away from Commie spies like Boris and Natasha in Prague and so that I won't forget my friend.

We skate up to the Brooklyn Bridge and then cross to the Esplanade and buy sodas from a vendor and eat and look at the city across the East River and promise each other that we will be roommates in college. It is a perfect day, and when it is over, the new wings on my feet carry me home.

I wake up with a start. In the gray light of early morning I see that Merry's sleeping bag is empty. My heart clutches and I start to get up, pulling my feet out from under Toby, but then I see her, sitting on the window seat, her forehead leaning against the sash of a window she has thrown open. She can't possibly fall—a previous owner installed a decorative metal grille outside the bank of windows running the length of our bedroom—but there is something solitary and sad about her silhouette against the window.

I hesitate, wondering if she wants company. Without getting up, Toby thumps her tail a few times, watching me, and that's invitation enough for me to sink back into my comfortable nest.

"You 'wake?" Merry asks, like she always does.

I sigh. You'd have thought it was still too early even for a morning person like my sister. "Uh-huh," I say, but in a discouraging sort of way.

"Last day," she says, pretending not to notice.

"Yup." Oh, all right. I stretch and sit up again, trying not to disturb Toby, who signals her disapproval by refusing to raise her head from her paws. The metallic gray of the early-morning light has drained the color from the room, lending it the quality of an old photograph.

"Do you remember the time Toby tried to jump out the window?" Merry asks me.

We had been going to spend the day at the vineyard. Everyone was getting in the station wagon when Cory yelled and pointed at something. We all twisted our heads and saw, seven stories above our heads, something wriggling and copper-colored struggling to free itself from the small space between an open window and the safety grille—a something that eventually resolved itself into Toby, who had seen the car and was doing everything she could to come with us.

It's not something I like to remember.

"I woke up this morning," Merry goes on, "and it seemed like that's what we're about to do. Jump out of our life. Except this time there won't be any bars to catch us."

A wave of relief washes away the cold, shimmering jelly that coats my brain. I thought I was alone in this.

She catches me looking at her and misinterprets the reason. She ducks her head, embarrassed. "I know I sound overdramatic. But that's kind of what it feels like. That we're walking off a cliff and don't yet see what's going to catch us."

I stand up, wrap myself in my sleeping bag, and go sit on the window seat, where I can prop my feet against hers.

"I know," I say.

We sit for a minute, looking out at the empty streets, our feet pressing together. I relax. My limbs get heavy.

"Mer," I say eventually.

"Yeah."

"It's, like, four in the morning."

"Yeah."

"I'm going back to sleep."

"Okay." But she doesn't move.

"Aren't you coming?"

She shakes her head, still staring out the window. "I don't want to miss the sun coming up."

"Why? You can't see it. All the buildings are in the way."

"I know," she says. "But you can see the gold light moving toward you down Eighty-ninth Street. I've always liked knowing that the light comes to find me every morning."

Good old Merry. Always sure the sun rises just for her. Most days I would be merciless, but today isn't most days. "Okay," I say, and go back to bed.

THE **SECOND** TIME

Six hours later, our life in the city is over.

I've been trying to plan for the hole I knew was coming. But it turns out that sometimes it takes a while to start missing something, because life just keeps on rolling along so fast that you can't see the holes until you are past them. New York is gone, but now the vineyard has come to take its place.

It's the first time since Presidents' Day that we've been to my grandparents' vineyard, because of my collarbone. There's a lot that needs doing, so Merry and I talk our way out of helping unpack and go straight to the fields. But now that we're here, I'm not being as productive as usual. Holding the secateurs bothers my shoulder a little, but that's just the excuse I have ready for Grandpop if he gives me a hard time. The real reason I'm not getting more done is that I keep stopping to look. I can't get enough of the view, hill after green hill rolling down to the Hudson. I love it here.

Almost as if my thought has summoned him, I hear the familiar beep-beep of the horn, and there's Grandpop, gesturing that he wants to talk to us. Merry and I look at each other, wipe off our secateurs and lock them closed, and make our way over to the service road, the mud from a really wet spring pulling at our big rubber boots like it doesn't want us to go.

"We don't need you in the vineyard today after all," he says. "I've come to take you back."

But it's a beautiful day, sunny and smelling of summer, and my eyes aren't full of the terraced vineyard yet. "I'm okay to stay here for a while," I say. "How about you, Mer?"

Grandpop looks sheepish. "Your grandmother wants you at the house," he says. "We've got a contractor coming to give us a bid on the remodel, and she needs you to polish up your rooms a little."

"What remodel?" Merry asks.

"The remodel of the guest cottage," he says.

"The what?" I say.

Grandpop looks back and forth between us. "Your mom hasn't told you?"

We shake our heads.

He gets a shifty look on his face. I think to myself, not believing it, that he is embarrassed. But he can't be. He's the grandfather. We're the kids. "Since you kids won't be around anymore, your Nana and I have decided to turn the cottage into a bed-and-breakfast."

"You're doing *what*?" I say, like maybe Grandpop didn't say the words I know he did.

"We're opening a bed-and-breakfast," Grandpop says. "It's something we've talked about for a long time. We didn't want to upset things when you guys were here, but now that you're leaving—well, your Nana is always looking for excuses to fuss with catalogs and wallpaper samples."

"I bet it's fun to be planning something new," Merry says. Her face looks like she means it, that she's really happy that they are taking away our house, the house we have spent every summer of our lives in. I must be seeing it wrong because everything seems upside down.

Grandpop smiles at her. "It is," he says. "Between curtains and carpets and I don't know what-all, your grandmother is having a field day."

Their faces zoom away and change and harden so that I see what they are like under their skin. I don't like the new faces. I try to call the old ones back.

"So you're saying we're not even going to be able to come stay with you?" I ask, trying to smile.

He looks at me, his face softening so that he looks like the old Grandpop. "Not at all, Jujube," he says, using my baby name. "You guys are welcome anytime. But the truth of the matter is that, after this summer, you just won't be here that often."

"So you and Nana need to do what's best for you," I say, testing him.

"Yes, I suppose so," he agrees slowly.

I turn away so I won't have to see the stranger that lives inside my Grandpop. He calls after me, "You want to drive us back to the house, sweetie?" but if I answered, he would be winning something. I ignore him, walk to the spigot at the end of the row, turn it on, and watch the water gush out.

"We're not even gone yet and they're changing everything around," I say as Merry joins me and we sluice the mud off our hands and boots.

"Grandpop said they've been thinking about this for a long time," Merry says. "It's only natural that once we're gone they'll make some changes."

"But it's not *right*," I say. "Grandparents aren't supposed to *do* that."

"Do what?"

"Put their own interests before their grandchildren's."

She scowls at me.

"Doesn't it *bother* you that other people are completely changing our lives? That there's nothing left?"

"Oh, come off it, Jude. Why are you making a federal case of this? I thought you'd be totally up for it."

"Well, I'm not."

I can hardly breathe.

By the time we get back to the house, I'm really angry. No, enraged. I *hate* it when Merry cops out. She always does this. She never lets herself see problems that upset the status quo. Doesn't she *get* what our grandparents are doing to us? They are kicking us out so that they can rent out our lives to some yuppies from the Upper West Side who will sleep in our beds and paw through the books we've left on our shelves and drink the wine from the grapes that we took care of, that we planted and pruned and watered and weeded and fertilized. It is so unfair that I think I will burst, but I don't, and the fury just keeps getting bigger and bigger. I want to scream and break things to let it out, like I did when I was a little kid and my arm would get stuck in the armhole of my coat.

Merry is vacuuming the little sitting room that adjoins our bedroom. I slam the door between the rooms so I can hear myself think. I look around the bedroom for something to break. Nothing. I jerk open my bureau drawers and paw through my stuff. Nothing. I knock everything off my desk. Nothing.

Wait. A black permanent marker.

I turn back to the bureau, its drawers still askew. My great-grandfather built it for his bride out of thick, hand-finished mahogany. It is one of my grandmother's most cherished possessions. Quickly I dump my clothes on the floor, and in large, angry letters on the bottom of every drawer I write: GO HOME!

A **PERFECT** AFTERNOON

I lie in bed, my limbs jumping a little as they settle into the mattress. Merry is reading one of Nana's women's magazines, *Good Housekeeping* or *Ladies' Home Journal* or something, in the bed next to mine. I have a book, too, but it can wait for tomorrow. The tree frogs down by the pond are chirping at the moon, and it is a lullaby my heavy body cannot resist.

"Mer," I say, having to make an effort to form the words, "turn out the light."

"In a minute," she says. I hear her turn another page; then she sighs. "Oh, all right." I hear the magazine slap down on the old mahogany table between our beds, just loud enough to show that she is doing this for me, not because she wants to, and then her light snaps off.

"Thanks," I say.

"Think nothing of it," she says. I hear the rustle of bed-clothes as she gets comfortable. "*God's in His heaven—All's right with the world*," she says. "Quote."

Robert Browning, "Pippa's Song," I think to myself, but I am too tired to say it as I slip toward sleep.

The frogs are very loud. Their chirps sound like honks. Fretful, I try to push the noise away, but I can't. Finally, disgusted, I throw back the covers and sit up. I look over to Merry's bed. She is lying with her head turned away from me, her figure still and relaxed in the silver moonlight. But the frog calls are getting louder and louder. Something is wrong.

I don't want to get up, but I know I must. I pad over to the window and peer out. *Everything is fine*, I tell myself.

But then, from the corner of my eye, I see it. A strange orange glow from the treehouse. At first I think it is someone smoking a cigarette, but no one here smokes. I look again, and see, not really believing it, that it is a pair of eyes. Then I pick out another pair, and another. With a sick jolt I realize that the tree frogs are not frogs but gremlins. The wind blows, and as branches move and toss, I see them riding among them, their sharp, strong nails stabbing deep into limbs of apple wood and Douglas fir.

They see that I have discovered them. One disengages from the tree, then another. Suddenly there is a swarm, heading straight for my bedroom window.

I slam it shut and turn to shake Merry awake. But her eyes, black and flat as stones, are open and watching me. "It's all right," I say, trying to reassure her, trying to keep her safe. "The window is strong. They won't get in." Behind me, I hear thumps and scrabbles as the swarm reaches the house, but I can't look away. She needs to know that I see her, that I will keep her safe.

But as I watch, her eyes begin to change. Horror claws at my throat as I see the terrible orange glow looking at me out of my sister's eyes. I try to scream, but there is no sound.

I'm standing by the kitchen sink in the guesthouse, examining the popped blisters on my hands. Dread has hovered around my shoulders ever since I shook myself awake early this morning. I tried to make it go away by working extra-hard, taking the vines and the sun inside my body as I pruned, and that helped. But then I couldn't stop thinking about how wearing leather gloves was like trapping my hands in dead animals, and I had to take them off. So I did. But my hands were city-soft, and now I've messed them up pretty good.

The screen door bangs and I jump, but it's just Merry, flushed and tired from four hours of pruning and intent on grabbing a soda from the fridge. I look back down at my weeping palms, then open the cabinet with my elbow and pull out a tube of first-aid cream and a bunch of Band-Aids. Once the blisters are washed, bound, and covered with gloves, I probably won't feel a thing. I unscrew the tube with my teeth and squeeze a line of cool white ointment onto my hands, but I can't stop a quick suck of air as the pain thrills through my hands and up my arms. I wait for it to subside, then reach for the Band-Aids.

Merry speaks from behind me, and I jump. "Your hands look *awful*," she says. "Told you you should have worn gloves. Mom's going to have a cow."

"Mom will never know," I say. It's hard to tear the Band-Aids open without smearing the cream. "They'll be fine in no time."

Merry drops her chin and gives me one of her looks, but she puts her root beer down, takes the bandages from me, opens them, and gently presses them onto my palms.

"Thanks," I say.

I hear Mom's quick footsteps in the upstairs hall. "Don't say anything," I hiss. I toss the wrappings in the garbage and jam my hands into my jean pockets as Mom's loafer-clad feet appear on the kitchen stairs.

Mom thumps a full laundry basket onto the table and yanks open the folding doors that screen the washer and dryer. She pulls out the dried clothes, plops them on top of the washer, and begins to fold them quickly and efficiently. "Your father and I thought it might be fun to take a picnic to the park in Peekskill." She nods toward the kitchen table, where the old red cooler is packed and waiting.

Merry and I look at each other.

"Since when do we go on picnics to Peekskill?" I ask.

"Since the plumbers called to say they had a cancellation and did Nana want them to come out this afternoon and begin work on Cory's room."

"What do the plumbers want with Cory's room?" I ask.

Mom's hands pause for a moment, and the dish towel she is folding flaps in the air like a white flag. Then she folds it quickly and stacks it in the pile with the others. "They've decided that the bedroom next to it needs a closet and an attached bathroom."

My body realizes what she has said before my mind has worked it out, so that fury is already pumping through my veins when I realize that she has just told me that Nana and

Grandpop are destroying Cory's bedroom for a toilet and a walk-in closet.

"They're getting rid of Cory's room before we have even *left*?" I say. I think of a wrecking ball crashing into Cory's closet and scattering the shelves of cowboy boots, every pair she has ever owned, carefully polished and lined up just so, covering them with bits of plaster and bent nails, smashing her memories and safe places. "They're just throwing her *out*?"

"No one is throwing anyone out of anywhere. Look, Jude, as I told Nana, this is their house, not ours, and they should do—"

"Where's Cory supposed to sleep now? In the vintage claw-foot bathtub Nana can't stop talking about?"

Mom presses her lips together and takes a breath before speaking. "Cory's going to sleep on the couch in the sitting room next to your bedroom, and I don't want to hear another word about it. This is hard for everyone, Jude, not just you, and it's time you pulled yourself together." She stacks the folded clothes and heads for the stairs to put them away.

"I'm not done yet!" I yell.

"Yes, you are," Mom says without turning around.

My parents are gone. They're in Prague, getting our apartment set up while we kids try to stay out of the way of the builders. There is nothing to show us what comes next, nothing to help us plan. I try not to think about how we're whizzing toward something we're not ready for. If I'm not working, I'm reading. All the books I read as a kid, over and over again, riding out on the prairie with Laura Ingalls and Little Britches, building space machines with Danny Dunn and Kip Russell. And when I get tired of that, I put on my rollerblades and holler for Cory and she puts on her regular roller skates and we go out skating on the back roads with Toby to keep us company. Cory loves skating as much as I do.

When I get my money on payday, we shut Toby in the kitchen and skate down to the station and take the 1:07 into the city, where we buy black-and-white cookies at the Grand Central Zabar's. Then we take the subway down to Paragon Sports.

When we climb out of the subway into Union Square Park, the heat and humidity slam into us, flavored with the stench of urine and dog poop. I've forgotten the way summer in the city sucks the life and energy right out of you, even in a park. A black man wearing filthy army fatigues is sitting slumped against a tree, his hand frozen in the air in front of his face. It's the kind of thing that really upsets Cory, but neither of us says anything. The waxed paper bag feels heavy in my hands. I make Cory wait while I go back and put the bag of cookies on the ground next to him in case he is hungry.

"What's wrong with him?" Cory whispers after we've gone half a block.

I shrug. "His brain doesn't work right."

"What will happen to him?"

"I don't know."

We walk for a little bit. "Do you think he'll be able to eat the cookies?" she says.

I shrug.

"Or do you think someone will come and steal them from him?"

"I really don't know, Cor." We cross the street.

"Do you think there are a lot of homeless people in Czechoslovakia?"

I think about it for a minute. "I think the Communists really like being organized and in charge of everything," I say. "I bet they have some system, special housing or something."

"That's what I think, too," says Cory.

We separate to walk around an old woman pulling a big old basset hound.

"Maybe Czechoslovakia won't be so bad after all," she says when we are together again.

"Maybe," I say. We are finally at Paragon, and I am glad to change the subject. "This is where Lexy bought me my blades. You want to go in?"

To my surprise, Cory hesitates. "I don't think so."

"What's wrong?"

She hesitates; then the words come out in a rush. "Seeing blades will just make me wish I had some."

I pull out my wallet. "Why do you think we're here?"

Cory looks at me and her eyes are so big they are practically circles. "You're going to buy me some blades?"

I grin at her. "Yep."

"Of my very own?"

"That's the plan," I say.

She looks like someone turned a light on inside her, and she doesn't even know what's coming up next. We're going to find a deli and buy ham sandwiches with mayo and lettuce on Kaiser rolls and a really good dessert. Then we will fly across the Brooklyn Bridge so we can talk and laugh and see the city from the Esplanade, because that's what makes a perfect afternoon.

CZECHOSLOVAKIA

August 1989

ARRIVAL

The first thing everyone said when we told them we were moving was, "Czechoslovakia? But that's behind the Iron Curtain!" I am old enough to know a metaphor when I hear one, but as Merry, Cory, and I stumble off the plane at Ruzyně Airport in Prague, the first thing I think is that all those people were right. Despite the August sun beating down on us, there seems to be a thin skin of cold, gray, dusty metal covering Czechoslovakia.

"I don't see Mom and Dad," Cory frets, hanging so tightly to my hand that I'm beginning to wonder about nerve damage.

"They can't see us until we've gone through Customs," Merry reminds her. "But it shouldn't take long. The airport doesn't look very busy."

"It's not very clean, is it?" Cory says.

I am tempted to tell her that she is no treat to look at herself, with her eyes gummy from sleep and one side of her hair doing a fair imitation of a magpie's nest. But then I realize that no one else is talking. No one. We're surrounded by people, but they are completely silent, even the babies.

The signs are useless—little hand-lettered things, grimy with age and written in Czech and Russian. I have no idea how to pronounce anything. Czech has American letters, but they're sprinkled with the upside-down pointed hats of diacritical marks. We follow what seems to be the largest stream of passengers and hope for the best.

Our footsteps echo weirdly through the silence. The light is different, too. It seems to drain the color out of things, like a piece of film that has been run through a projector too many times, and it tastes of smoke.

I feel like we've stumbled onto the set of one of the old black-and-white movies that Grandpop watches when he can't sleep, *The Spy Who Came In from the Cold* or something. The impression is heightened when we pass a couple of guards with machine guns that are so blocky and awkward that they look like they were cobbled together from scrap lumber by an incompetent prop master.

"It sure is different here," Cory says.

"Yeah, but the people are just like us. I thought they'd be stoutly built with lots of cheekbones and squinty eyes and kerchiefs," Merry says.

That's what's creepy. It's different, but not in the way you expect. It's like an easy chair that looks perfectly comfortable, maybe even inviting, until you actually sit in it and discover that, under its skirted slipcover, it's missing a leg.

At first glance, everyone seems remarkably normal. It is true that an unusual number of adults are wearing cheap plastic jellies like little girls playing dress-up. But something is awry. It takes me a minute to realize what it is: in this huge crowd, there's not a single dark face. Or fat body. Nor is there even the tiniest hint of expression to be found on all those polite, blank faces. "This is a Stepford airport," I say. "Populated by robots."

"In that case, someone needs to reprogram the baggage handlers," Merry says, nodding toward the baggage claim, which is nothing but a pile of luggage dumped willy-nilly on the concourse.

We somehow manage to make it through Customs without provoking an international incident, despite the fact that I have smuggled in the fall education issue of the *New York Times* for Dad. But we must seem harmless; a young official who smells like it's been a while since he's seen the inside of a shower waves us through the checkpoint without bothering to open anything.

And there, finally, is Mom. We throw ourselves at her like shipwrecked sailors making for land.

"Where's Daddy?" Cory asks after we've gotten ourselves sorted out.

"He's right outside," Mom says. "We brought the school car for the luggage—it's bigger than the Volvo—but he was worried that if we parked it, we'd come back to find the hubcaps gone."

We drag the luggage out and find Dad standing guard over a sleek and shiny Mercedes-Benz that's about three times the size of the dirty cars that everyone else is getting into. "Way to go, Dad," Merry says admiringly. "Corrupt capitalist perks in a Communist state! How did you manage it?"

"*This* is nothing," Dad says, trying to peel Cory off his legs so he can come hug the rest of us. "Wait until you see the chauffeur. A real uniform and everything."

"Where is he?" Cory wants to know.

Dad makes a grand gesture. "We left him at home. We didn't want you to get the wrong impression—think we'd forgotten where we came from, that kind of thing."

"I don't believe that for a minute," Merry says. "You were just afraid that if he saw all of us at once he'd quit."

"You're on to me," Dad says, and ruffles Merry's hair. She hates that. "So, girls, how was the trip?"

We load everything into the huge trunk of the Mercedes while the five of us talk at the same time. Once we're all in and trying to figure out which seatbelt belongs to who, Dad turns around in his seat and clears his throat in a serious-head-of-school-I'm-not-kidding-and-there-will-be-a-test sort of way. We quiet down in a hurry, even Cory.

"Listen, girls, there are a couple of things we should discuss before we do anything else." He clears his throat again and pushes his glasses up with his finger, a mannerism that every Thatcher student has imitated at least once.

"First, some ground rules. Since the relationship between the United States and Czechoslovakia is tense, interactions between Americans and Czechoslovakian nationals are a little tricky. If I worked at the embassy, I would have to fill out a report every single time I talked to a Czech national, even if it was just to ask directions. Fortunately, I don't, and neither does your mother, so our family has a little more freedom than most others. But it's important for you to understand right up front that you will not be doing a Czech person any favors if you approach them in the street or become too closely involved with them."

"So we've come all this way and now we're not supposed to talk to anyone?" I say, disbelieving.

"Of course you can talk to people," Mom says. "There will be lots of them at school and at the embassy."

"But no actual Czechs," I say.

Mom sighs. "Not many, no."

I think of how much it has cost us to come to this place. What it was like to walk through that airport after all the hours on planes, worrying about connections and passports and tickets and reassuring Cory for the seven millionth time that just because she couldn't see anything holding up the plane didn't necessarily mean that we were doomed to a fiery death. Not to mention the packing and cleaning that had been going on for months. The inconvenience to my grandparents. Outrage, hot and bracing as the Irish coffee Nana pours for Grandpop after he's plowed the driveway, pours through me. "Why have we done this, then?" I say. "Why did we come all this way if we're not even supposed to talk to an actual Czechoslovakian person?"

"Jude," Dad says in a warning voice. "In a perfect world, these precautions wouldn't be necessary, but the bottom line is that your actions may have consequences that you don't anticipate. We all have to be extra-careful not to put anyone in an uncomfortable position."

"So in other words, we're under house arrest." I wriggle

my shoulders, finding it hard to breathe in this shiny car that is so full of people. I roll down the window, but the stifling sights and smells of a strange new place are even more suffocating. I have to move. I have to get away. But there's nowhere to go.

Dad's eyes lock onto me in the rearview mirror. "Listen carefully," Dad says.

I am listening carefully. I am listening to his voice, which somehow makes room for air in my lungs.

"Jude. We are serious."

I start to say something, but he won't let me.

"I know this is hard for you, but I need your word on this. *You* may think it's simple politeness to invite someone home or to give away your things to someone who looks like they need them, but they will not thank you for it when they're dragged in for questioning for fraternizing with an American spy. And the repercussions could be equally serious for the rest of us. I don't mean to be overdramatic, but the stakes are high on this one."

He sounds so ridiculous that I realize this can't possibly be happening in real life. Dad, if he were really Dad, would never talk as though he were a character in a B movie. It's a bad dream. Everyone else thinks it's real, but I know it is not. It's not real, so it's not serious. It's just a dream. All I have to do is play along until it is over.

"Are we all clear on this?" Dad insists, still watching me in his mirror.

I promise. But it doesn't count, because none of this makes sense.

Dad starts the car and we pull away, driving down a pot-holed road that takes us farther into the heart of the fantastic dream that has decided to come visit me. We pass an old grandmother dressed all in black and bent beneath a load of firewood, stumping along the road like a refugee from a fairy tale. Then a guy in a bright blue coverall swinging a scythe—or maybe a sickle: the one with the really long handle so you don't have to bend over—to cut grass. Then the housing projects start. All of them look exactly alike: tall boxes of crumbling cement with rows of windows marching across each floor like ants.

"Are we going to live in one of *those*?" Cory asks in a little voice.

"No, honey," Mom says. "The government has special apartments for foreigners. Ours is actually quite nice. I think you'll like it."

As we get closer to the city, the buildings shrink down to a more manageable size. They are crumbling and dirty, but behind the overgrown trees and uncut grass of their neglected gardens, you can see that some of them must have been pretty nice once.

"Do we live right downtown?" Merry asks.

"Nope," says Dad. "We're across the river in Dejvice. It's been built up only in the last hundred years, so the houses tend to be a bit more spacious and in better repair than the ones in the historical center."

"The school's in Dejvice, too," Mom says. "Not far from the residence of the American ambassador."

"So the soldiers can protect us?" Cory asks.

"No," says Dad. "We don't need protecting. Prague is very, very safe. Even at night." He turns the car down a narrow street that leads into a leafy little square, pulls over to the curb, and kills the engine. "This is it!" he says. "Everybody out!"

We unfold ourselves and emerge from the car, yawning and stretching.

To be honest, it's a lot better than I was afraid it might be. The buildings here are not elegant, but they look comfortable and they have lots of windows. A small public garden to one side of the square overlooks the Vltava River and the historical center.

"This reminds me of Brooklyn Heights," Merry says.

Mom snaps her fingers. "That's it!" she says. "I knew it reminded me of something, but I couldn't put my finger on what. It's been driving me crazy." She slings one arm around Merry and the other around me. "Oh, how I've missed my girls," she says, and hugs us hard.

"How about some help here?" Dad calls. We hustle over and he loads us all up while Mom unlocks the front door of the apartment building with a big, old-fashioned brass key. The lobby smells of coal and dust and is covered in faded wallpaper that looks at least sixty years old, but it's big with a high ceiling and it opens onto an overgrown courtyard in the back.

There's a rickety-looking elevator to one side like the one in *Charade*. Cory heads for it, but Mom says, "Out of order, honey. For the last five or six years, according to the lady upstairs."

"We're just going to the second floor," Dad says, puffing in the door with four suitcases.

"Should I stay with the car?" Merry asks.

"It should be okay for a few minutes," Dad tells her.

We follow Mom up a flight of fancy stone steps to a landing with two doors. One of them has a splintery wooden table outside of it with a tray of dusty-looking plants. The other door is hung with a tile painted with the words *Pax et bonum*, "Peace and comfort," which Mom and Dad bought in Assisi on their honeymoon, and I know that we are home.

The door opens onto more pleasant surprises. Light streams into the living room through big, old-fashioned windows and reflects off fancy plaster carvings on the ceilings and etched glass panels set in the French doors that lead to the bedrooms. The furniture is big and heavy and comfortably upholstered in luxurious fabrics, like something you'd expect to find in the home of someone's French *grandmère*. Merry is beside herself with delight, especially after Mom and Dad show her our bedroom, which has a beautiful view of Prague Castle. Cory's bedroom looks down on the overgrown little courtyard in back. The three of us have to share a bathroom, but it's huge, big enough for a regular-size washer and dryer along with an old-fashioned claw-foot bathtub that Nana would have a fit over, mirrors, a toilet, and a bidet, which Mom has to explain to us.

"Just so you don't expect us to use it on a regular basis," I say.

"It's very handy for washing out stockings," Mom says.

Merry runs her hand over the smooth, gleaming tiles set

into the wall. "So what happened to all those shoddy Russian appliances with faulty wiring you kept warning us about?"

"You forget that we have come up in the world," Dad says. "As headmaster of the International School I am technically an employee of the State Department, which means I have a diplomatic passport and can go back and forth to Germany anytime I want to get whatever we need."

"Did you guys do all this yourself?" I ask, impressed. Neither one of them is what you would call handy.

"Oh, no," Mom says. "That was the family before us. She taught math and he was in the consulate at the embassy. But I did put in that light fixture."

We watch while she demonstrates, flipping the light switch on and off. It looks like an ordinary light fixture, but she seems proud of having done it, so we all make admiring sounds.

"The instruction booklet was in German," she explains. "It took me about a week to figure it out, but then I ran around the apartment singing, 'I am woman, hear me roar.' Who knows what the StB thought."

"The who?"

Mom hesitates. Dad looks at her and shrugs.

"The StB are the state police," Mom says. "Since we are foreigners, they have probably bugged our apartment."

"They *what*?" Cory says.

Dad lifts Cory onto the washing machine so that they are eye to eye. "The Communists want to make sure no one is doing anything that will hurt the government," he says. "So they put bugs—little microphones—in the buildings that they let foreigners live in, and they tape what they say. But it's nothing to worry about. No one has time to listen to all those tapes, so they pay attention to them only if one of us does something that makes them suspect that we might be dangerous. As long as you behave sensibly, the bugs won't matter. And after a while you'll get used to them and forget they are even here."

"So people are going to be listening to us all the time?" Cory absolutely hates to cry and she's stretching her eyes open so she won't, but you can see the tears anyway.

"I can't imagine that anyone is going to listen to boring people like us," Mom says. "Now, there's a back-to-school picnic at ISC at five o'clock. I'm going to make us something to eat before Dad has to leave for the office, and then let's see if we can finish unpacking before it's time to get ready. You'll want to look your best when you meet your new friends."

The school's chauffeur, Jaroslav, picks us up for the picnic. Here at last is Merry's stoutly built Czechoslovakian. He's in his late fifties and with no neck or hair to speak of. He is also very correct, with white gloves and a ridiculous little chauffeur's cap that looks like Popeye's sailor hat.

He ushers us into the Mercedes-Benz. "So. You are good, madam? You have your seatbelts on, dear children?"

"Yes, thank you, Jaroslav," Mom says. "We're all set."

He eases away from the curve with as much care as if we were made of spun glass.

"Dad's going to meet us there, right, Mom?" Cory says for the third time.

"Yep," Mom says.

"You are just arrived?" Jaroslav asks us.

"Yes, this morning," Merry says politely.

"So you have not seen much of our city?"

"Not yet," Merry says. "But we hope to soon."

"Then I show you where your ambassador lives," Jaroslav says. He makes a quick turn, then another, and then we pull up to a huge mansion set well back behind a tall iron fence and watched over by the biggest American flag I have ever seen.

"Ambassador Shirley Temple Black," he says with relish. "You have seen her movies?"

"Who?" says Cory.

"Shirley Temple, the little actress. She sang 'On the Good Ship Lollipop.'"

We shake our heads.

"I think she was a little before their time," Mom says.

He shakes his head. "Too bad. She is one hot tomato."

I see that Merry is biting back a smile. "Where did you learn your English?" she asks him. "It's excellent."

"I drove a jeep for Americans in the war," he says. "Nice house, huh?" We admire it obediently. "It was built by a Czech industrialist," he says.

"He must have been very rich," Cory says.

"Many people were rich then," Jaroslav says, and starts the car moving again.

"Czechoslovakia was quite a wealthy country at one point," Mom says. "Particularly between the time she got her independence in 1918 and Hitler's invasion in 1938."

"Czechoslovakia wasn't invented until 1918?" Cory asks.

"Well, Czechs have been living here for more than a thousand years," Mom says. "But for most of that time it was part of Austria."

"And they only had their own country for twenty years before Hitler and then the Communists?" Cory says. "That's so sad."

Mom stiffens slightly and nods toward Jaroslav. Oops.

But if Cory's words threaten the balance of American–Czechoslovakian relations, Jaroslav doesn't seem to notice. He turns the car onto a narrow lane and brings it to a stop in front of a big, old white house. "So. We have arrived," he says, and jumps out to open the passenger door for us.

The school is nothing like the ambassador's elegant residence. It looks like the kind of place a huge Victorian family would live, with lots of porches and bay windows and nooks and crannies. It takes me a minute to notice the discreet bronze sign, in English, that reads WELCOME TO THE INTERNATIONAL SCHOOL OF CZECHOSLOVAKIA.

"There's Dad's office," Mom says, pointing to a bay window. Behind us, Jaroslav drives off and two other big, black Mercedes-Benzes draw up to take his place. Between them they discharge about fifteen dark-skinned children of varying sizes accompanied by two men in robes and tasseled caps.

I walk a few steps away to scope out the playground situation. It's a good-sized yard for a house, and they've put in a slide and some swings and stuff, but if anyone plays team sports at ISC, they don't do it here.

I wander back to the fam in time to see another Benz unloading a well-dressed man who looks American or British, his beautiful Indian wife, wearing a sari in the August heat, and their two children—a boy a year or two older than Merry and me, and a girl about Cory's age.

"This really is an international school, isn't it?" Mom says.

"Too bad none of them are actually Czech," I say.

"Don't any Czech kids go here?" Cory asks.

Mom shakes her head. "No one from the Eastern Bloc," she says. Then, in an obvious attempt to change the subject, she points to a bunch of casually dressed men coming out the back door of the neighboring villa. "Can you guess who they are?"

They are all young with very short haircuts. "Missionaries!" Cory cries.

"No, sweetheart, not in Czechoslovakia," Mom says.

We watch them fan out across the villa's backyard, which is higher and flatter than the school's. Two of them pull out cans of spray paint and begin to paint boundaries on the grass, while another drops some rubber things that are apparently meant to be bases. More young men bring out bats and a plastic bucket of balls and another of gloves, and some of the older kids who are milling around the school's yard, drinking what looks like watery Kool-Aid and eating cookies, wander over.

"What are they doing?" I ask Mom.

"It looks to me like they are choosing up sides for softball," Mom says.

"I thought we weren't supposed to fraternize," I say.

"We're not. That's the DCM's house, and those guys are off-duty marines," Mom explains. "There's not much for them to do, so whenever the school has a party or anything, they usually invite the marines along."

"That's the what's house?"

"The DCM's—the deputy chief of mission. The ambassador's righthand man," Dad says, coming up behind us. He gives Mom a quick kiss. "Jaroslav found you all right? You guys want to go play?"

"C'mon, Mer. It'll be fun," I say.

"No thanks," she says, like she doesn't really care one way or the other. But I know better. For all that she's more tuned in to social things than I am, Merry is easily overwhelmed by large groups. Plus she's truly terrible at sports.

"Aw, c'mon," I wheedle.

"I don't think so."

"Looks like they could use you," Dad says.

But Merry can be stubborn when she wants to, so finally Cory and I go off without her. It's a great game. Cory catches a pop fly and I hit a homer and make a double play. They make Dad come over and pitch the last inning. If you saw him on the street you'd take him for a wimpy intellectual who throws like a girl, but he's a really good pitcher.

After the game, we meet our homeroom teachers and classmates and get sheets to tell us what to bring the first day of school. There aren't enough kids in each grade, so they're grouped together. The elementary school has just two classes, and the middle school and the upper school have one each. Merry and I check out the roster for our sophomore/junior/

senior class, and discover that there are only seven kids in it. Seven. Including us.

"Yeah, it's pretty small even for ISC," Mr. Lundquist, our homeroom teacher, tells us. "But a lot of diplomats have been getting PNG'd lately."

Merry and I look at each other, puzzled, and the Indian boy we saw getting out of the car explains. "PNG stands for *persona non grata.* The West is putting a lot of pressure on the regime to honor the human-rights stuff they agreed to at the Helsinki Accords, and every time the regime is embarrassed they throw someone else out. It's really cutting into the school's population."

Merry gives me a look that says, "Toto, I've got a feeling we're not in Kansas anymore," and I give a slow blink of acknowledgment before stepping forward and sticking out my hand. "Hi," I say. "I'm Jude Wheelock. This is my sister Merry."

"Wheelock. Are you related to …"

"Yeah. He's our dad. And we've got a sister, Cory, in fourth grade," I say.

"Me, too," he says. "Her name's Kate. I'll tell her to keep an eye out for Cory. My name's Sunil Montgomery, and I'm a junior. What about you guys?"

"We're sophomores," I say.

"Are you twins?" he asks, surprised, looking back and forth between us.

"Fraternal," I say.

A rangy, dark-skinned girl standing next to me giggles. "My name is Abebi," she says. "You have a great arm, Judy."

"Jude," I correct her.

"Like *Jude the Obscure*," says an American boy with blond hair, a tennis sweater, and horn-rimmed glasses. "I'm Freeman Lattimore. My mom is the Cultural at the embassy."

Abebi, who's from Nigeria, is a sophomore. Sunil, whose father is a Canadian diplomat, and Freeman are juniors. Ahmed, a plump oil kid from Jordan, and Sophy, a French girl who is furious that her parents haven't sent her to boarding school in Switzerland, are seniors.

They're all curious about us—in such a small school, any new blood must be welcome—but Merry and I have hit the wall. We are both so exhausted that we're slurring our words. It's a huge relief when Mom scoops us up and pours us into the Mercedes. We're asleep before Jaroslav can get the car turned around.

Creatures are looming outside. I can't really see them, which is the worst part. I just catch glimpses of furry legs, wet teeth in red gums, coyote ears, green and orange eyes. But I know that they are here because of me.

I am trying to keep them out. But I am in the school, and I don't know it well. I keep finding new rooms, and all of them have trap doors and windows ajar to the outside. I lock and latch one opening after another while the creatures hurl themselves against the doors with soft thumps and whimpers. It finally occurs to me that I don't need to keep them out of the whole house, just out of the room I am in. I find the room with the stoutest doors. It is a library with a huge fireplace. I bolt the doors, start a huge fire, and take refuge in a big leather chair like Grandpop's to wait until morning when Dad will come to work and find me. I sit in the chair, my limbs getting heavier and heavier with tiredness until I know they have stopped working as surely as if they were tied to the chair with chains. But it doesn't matter, because the doors are bolted and the windows are too high for the creatures to get to.

Just as I am about to fall asleep, I feel it. A little flutter in my chest. It's not unpleasant. Just a little flutter, like a tired muscle twitching. The twitches get stronger until they are nibbles. I don't understand where the feeling is coming from. I pull up my shirt to see my stomach, and it looks the same as ever. Then it starts to ripple.

The nibbles become nips, then bites. The ripples turn into one large bump, and then another, straining outside from my stomach. Pain explodes as my flesh tears. A snout pushes out, then green and orange eyes, coyote ears, a hairy paw. The creature is in me. How can I keep it away if it is in me? I scream, but the scream sounds like a howl.

I'm awake, lying in my bed, panting. Where am I? I'm not in my bedroom in New York. That doesn't belong to us anymore. I'm not in my bedroom at Nana and Grandpop's. That's getting turned into a B&B. *Where am I?* I look out the window and see Prague Castle looming above me like a black prison in the silver light.

Prague. We're in Prague. I look over to the other side of the room. Merry is there, sleeping peacefully. I taste the fear of the dream in my mouth and I want to wake her up, but I don't.

I turn away, untangling myself from my sweaty sheets. It was just a dream. Just a dream. I turn my pillow over, looking for a cool, dry surface. I want Toby, who is home chasing chipmunks at Nana and Grandpop's. I lie still, my eyes closed, counting my breaths, making them longer and longer. It was just a dream, a dream, a dream.

Slowly, gently, a rough tongue rasps across the inside of my stomach.

I'm here, it says. *I'm with you.*

It's just a dream.

THE **DEMONSTRATION**

Mom and Dad have a parent cocktail party late Sunday afternoon at the school and a big Fulbright party that evening at the American Embassy, so we don't have to go to church. That's a good thing, since the nearest Mormon branch is at the American base in Nuremberg, and we've already had to drive all the way out there once this week for school supplies.

Instead of church, Mom and Dad decide to take us on a little orientation walk through Prague. The five of us walk along the cracked and pitted sidewalk. After a block or two we get to the woods of Castle Hill. I take a deep breath to smell the pines. But all I can smell is smoke.

The woods lead up past the Belvedere, the summer palace, to the back entry of Prague Castle, both guarded by men in uniform holding those same fake-looking guns we saw at the airport. I keep thinking that I hear music, and then it fades away again.

Now I can definitely hear music. The breeze is bringing

it to me to make up for the woods that smell of smoke. The breeze hovers around me, lifting my hair and blowing my T-shirt against me.

"Why are all the windows covered with plywood like that?" Cory asks. "Was there a fire?"

"That's where President Husak has his office," Dad says. "They've probably covered up the windows for security reasons."

"That's one ramshackle castle, if you ask me," Merry says. "It's got 'service project' written all over it."

"Come look at the cathedral," Mom says, leading us through an archway. "It's really something."

She's right. Saint Vitus Cathedral stands inside one of the castle's huge courtyards, bristling with spires and mosaics and statues just like a cathedral should. The sun bounces off the blackened stone, edging every line and texture and curve with light until my eyes can't hold any more and I have to look away.

We go out another way, past a chamber orchestra playing on a balustrade that overlooks the city, and clatter down wide stone steps built into the hill. Merry thinks this would be a great place to reenact the "Do-Re-Mi" scene from *The Sound of Music*. Fortunately, she's the only one who thinks it.

We wind our way along cobblestone streets as steep and narrow as paved goat paths, incongruously lined by Baroque mansions with dingy, peeling paint, until we get to the American Embassy. It's closed, of course, because it's Sunday, but Mom and Dad want us to know how to find it if we need it.

It is built against a wooded hill that reminds me of the woods behind Nana and Grandpop's farm. Somehow Dad knows that I need to be on that hill. There is a fence that keeps us from it here, but he knows another way, a little farther past the West German Embassy. And there it is—a secret path that takes us into the woods.

As we enter, the living smell of leaves and water curves around us like a hug. We walk on beaten earth past iron grillwork that borders the fancy backyards of the embassies. Some chipmunks skitter down the side of a tree and up the wooded hill on the right, and it's almost like playing spies in Central Park.

Mom shows us the place where Americans can plant gardens of their own behind our embassy. It's too late for this year, but we can get a plot next spring. In the winter, kids go sledding here, between pear and apple trees like the ones in Nana and Grandpop's backyard.

We wander slowly down to the Vltava River. "I'm *huuunn-gry*," Cory whines.

"Okay," Dad says. "Get out your maps. I want you to figure out what trams will take us across the river and where we can pick them up."

We get out at the National Theater, which looks like a dressed-up version of the Plaza Hotel with a gilded roof. Mom's in teacher mode now, and goes on and on about how it is this big symbol of the Czech national revival. "The whole country, peasants and everyone, gave money to build it, and then it burned down just before it opened. It meant so much to them that they did it all again. It's really kind of interesting—

when the Czechs lost their political leaders and nobility after the Battle of White Mountain in 1620, they turned to their artists and intellectuals for leadership—"

"I'm *huuunn*-gry," Cory says again.

"Me, too," Merry says.

"Me, three," Dad says.

"Wenceslas Square is just a block or two farther, and I thought we'd grab a hot dog there. Look at these buildings, kids. You can see how wealthy Czechoslovakia was at the beginning of the century. And how willing to experiment with new, more streamlined looks that didn't echo Habsburg—"

"Ginny," Dad says. "It's time for lunch."

"Okay, okay."

"We're not *buying* lunch, are we?" says Cory, scandalized. "It's the *Sabbath!*"

Mom looks guilty. "I know, honey," she says. "And we won't do it often. But Dad and I are both about to get very busy and it's just this once."

"*I'm* not going to eat anything that has to be bought on Sunday," Cory says.

"Okay," Mom says. "It's up to you, sweetheart."

We walk along National Street, which is wide and full of empty, dusty plate-glass windows, until we come out at the bottom of Wenceslas Square. There, way up at the top, King Wenceslas sits on a bronze horse watching over his people.

Even though all the stores are closed, there are still plenty of people walking up and down, window-shopping and enjoying the brilliant blue sky. We stop at a stand and buy enormous hot dog/sausage things that we slather with brown mustard. They remind me a little bit of New York hot dogs, the kind you buy in Central Park that crackle when you bite into them. Dad buys one for Cory, too, and she's halfway through it before she remembers she has Moral Scruples.

We fill ourselves with the hot dogs and bottled water and make our way to Good King Wenceslas. I was his page one year in a holiday pageant at school. I had to get tired and cold and crouch down on the stage until he rescued me.

A lot of people—maybe fifty—have also come to see the statue. Merry, who is out in front, slows down and looks at Dad. "I didn't think they allowed demonstrations in Communist countries," she says.

"They don't," Dad says.

"It sure looks like one to me," Merry says.

She is right. The crowd is milling around while some of them make speeches, and people on the sidewalk stop to watch.

"Damn!" Dad says suddenly. "It's the anniversary. I should have remembered."

"What anniversary?" I ask.

"The anniversary of the Russian invasion of Czechoslovakia in 1968," Dad says. "I don't understand," he adds, half to himself, "why the police haven't shut this down."

"I'm going to check it out," I say, and take off toward the crowd. Dad calls after me, but I ignore him.

By the time they catch up with me, I have crossed the cobblestone no-man's-land between the onlookers and the demonstrators, who are mostly kids just a little older than me.

The atmosphere is electric—like at the U2 concert Lexy took me and Merry to for our birthday last December—and I am all charged up.

"Jude," Mom says, tugging on my arm. "This isn't safe."

"What are they here for?" I ask. "What do they want?"

A shaggy young man turns around. "You are Americans?" he asks in an accent that is a funny combination of Czech- and British-sounding English.

"Yeah," I say. "My name is Jude."

"Judith!" Dad barks.

I ignore him.

"It's the twenty-first anniversary of the Soviet invasion," the young man says. "The Soviets killed a boy, just here, with a bayonet through the lungs. We have come today because we do not forget."

I stare at him, and for a moment he is the boy, with blood bubbling from his chest and the corner of his mouth. I look again, and he is whole. "Won't the police come and get you?"

The young man shrugs. "They are already here. They pretend to be protesters, just like us. They take our photographs. They talk to us so they can find what we are planning next."

"They're taking our photograph?"

The shaggy young man nods to the buildings on either side of the square. "They have offices up there," he says.

I feel energy pouring into my body until everything—my brain, my muscles, my hearing—is supercharged.

"It's not a good idea for us to be here," Mom says in a clipped voice. "Come on, girls."

"I'm not done!" I say.

"Yes, you are," Mom says, grabbing my arm so hard that it hurts.

"I think you're very brave," I tell the young man.

"Not brave," he says. "Just desperate."

"Take care," I say.

"And you," he replies.

Mom and Dad hurry us past the demonstration, heading to the subway stop at the National Museum. "We shouldn't have done this, Whit," Mom says.

"Don't worry, Ginny," Dad says. "Nothing happened."

"They can't do anything to us," I say. "We have diplomatic passports."

"That's the kind of thinking that can get you in real trouble," Dad says sharply.

When we get home, Mom and Dad head for their room to get ready for the Fulbright party. Mom comes into our room forty minutes later, all dolled up and fastening an earring.

"I've put a casserole in the oven and Jell-O in the fridge," she says. "Listen for the timer—it should go off at about five-thirty. Jude, you've got the dishes. Merry, you've got baths and prayers. Claudia said the party might go pretty late, so don't worry if we're not here by bedtime."

"Okay," I say.

"Merry, I told Cory she could stay up until nine now that she's going into fourth grade, but if you can get her in earlier that would be great. Tomorrow's a big day!"

"Okay, Mom," Merry says. "We will."

Mom pauses for a minute. "I hate to leave you like this the night before school starts," she says.

"Don't worry about it, Mom," I say. "We'll be fine. Go and have a good time."

Dad comes up behind her and kisses the back of her neck, and she giggles. "You guys be good," Dad says. "We might be pretty late."

"I was just telling them that," Mom says. "Hang on, Whit, I just want to say goodbye to Cory."

Dad steps into the room. "Cory seems a little tense," he says. "Maybe you guys could do something to take her mind off things—a game of Monopoly or something."

Cory does seem a little tense, so I decide to make a chocolate cake for dessert. Cory loves chocolate cake. Then I remember that she likes flying saucers even more. So we all sit around the big wooden table in the kitchen and play Monopoly. I dig around in the study until I find Mom's cassette player and I set it up and get a pile of tapes and we crank all our favorites—Carole King and James Taylor and Elvis Costello and the Bangles. When it's not my turn, I am stirring up a chocolate cake and pouring it into circles on the cookie sheets and baking the flying saucers one sheet at a time, since the casserole is on the other rack.

When the timer goes off and the casserole is ready to eat, I see that Mom has forgotten to make whipped cream for the Jell-O. So I make some in another bowl. Then, when the flying saucers have cooled, I make some buttercream frosting in another bowl and start sticking the flying saucers together. Merry is trying on outfits for the first day of school tomorrow.

She keeps coming in from the bedroom so we can tell her if she looks fat or not. We keep telling her that she looks fine, but I guess she doesn't believe us because she keeps sighing and going off to try on something else.

Since it's the day before school starts, I let Cory have as many flying saucers as she wants. I get her a tall glass of frosty-cold milk and change which square she's on when she's not looking so that she will have a better shot at landing on Free Parking and winning lots of money.

After a while, the game gets boring. I check the clock. It's only 7:45. I go look for Merry to see if she'll take my place for a while. She's asleep on her bed, surrounded by every article of clothing we possess.

It's still *light* outside, for crying out loud.

"Hey, Cory, you want to throw a ball around downstairs for a few minutes?" I say.

"Okay," she says.

We go downstairs and play catch in the park in front of our house, but it doesn't really help.

"Hey, Cor, you want to go see what happened at that demonstration?" I say. "It'll take, like, five minutes on the tram."

"No," she says.

"Come on, Cory. It'll be great," I coax.

"No, it won't," she says. "There are policemen there and they will take our picture."

"But we have diplomatic passports," I say.

Cory keeps shaking her head. "No," she says.

"Well, if you don't want to come, you don't have to," I say. "I just thought it would be safer with two of us."

That gets her. But she says, "We're not supposed to go."

"Guess you're not so brave after all," I say to the ball as I throw it up and catch it. I check her face out of the corner of my eye.

She looks stricken. "I'm brave," she says.

I catch the ball and take my mitt off. "Then come with me," I say. "C'mon. We'll take the tram over the bridge. And if we see anything that looks even a little dangerous, we just won't get off."

She hesitates.

"It's still really early," I say. "We'll be back in half an hour. You'll be in bed on time and everything."

"You promise we'll stay out of anything that looks like trouble?"

"Cross my heart," I say. "Honest."

"And I'm the one who gets to say if it looks like trouble?"

"Absolutely."

But she still hesitates.

"I'll pick you for my side in soccer for a month," I promise.

Fifteen minutes later our tram is halfway across the bridge to the National Theater when it stops. The driver says something over the loudspeaker that makes all the other passengers look annoyed. She opens the doors and they start to get off.

We sit there for a minute, but there is nothing we can do, so we get up, too. "Can you believe the way they just get off without complaining or anything?" I say to Cory, trying to distract her from thinking about whether this might be dangerous. "Can you imagine what they'd say in New York?"

"What's wrong?" she says, looking scared.

"I'm sure it's nothing," I say.

We get off the tram to see a large crowd milling around on the other side of the bridge, at least a thousand people. There are a lot of cars and vans and motorcycles stopped on the bridge, and I tug Cory between a rusty turquoise Škoda and two dingy white vans so we can see what's happening.

But the way is still blocked, by some big square vehicles I don't really look at because I want to see what's on the other side.

What's on the other side is policemen, hundreds of them. Some have truncheons and some of them have big dogs, which they handle casually, as if they were ordinary people holding newspapers and poodles. Except for an occasional muffled yelp from one of the dogs, everyone is spookily quiet and still. Their whole attention is on the crowd in front of the National Theater, who are being beaten.

Most of the marchers are sitting or lying down on the cobblestones, shielding their faces and heads as best they can from the sticks and the dogs.

Cory is scared, really scared.

"Let's go home," she says, her face white.

I look again. At first I think some of the demonstrators are helping to beat their friends up, but then I realize that the guys with the sticks must be the plainclothesmen the shaggy young man told us about earlier in Wenceslas Square.

It is eerily quiet. I've heard about the crack of a bat on a skull, but in real life it makes a dull, muffled sound. The crowd is mostly quiet, too. Some of them are moaning, and every once in a while someone yells in protest, but most of them have just sort of given in. They are so passive that I have to keep reminding myself that these are people who are being beaten, not dummies, and that the blood trickling down their faces is the real thing.

Cory makes a little sound and starts to back away, her hands over her mouth. I look to see what she has seen. The shaggy young man from Wenceslas Square is coming straight for us, carrying an injured girl whose blond hair is matted and darkened with blood. For some reason the police line parts to let him through, and he walks straight up the bridge toward us. I think they must realize we are Americans by the way we are dressed, and gratitude wells up in me that we are here so that we can help this girl.

I am starting forward when the shaggy young man gets too close to the side of the bridge and lets the girl's head clunk against the stone balustrade like it's a block of wood. I see that his face is as blank as those of the policemen standing around watching. He's StB. He must be StB. Cory's hand is somehow in mine and we shrink back against the bridge, away from the smell of his unwashed body, but he is so intent on getting his burden to the paddy wagon that he doesn't notice us.

When Cory turns and runs, I am right behind her.

THE **FIRST** DAY

Mom wakes us up the way she does on the first day of school every year. She sings, "Good marnin', good marnin', it's great to stay up late, good marnin', good marnin', to you," and pretends to be Debbie Reynolds tap-dancing in *Singin' in the Rain*. I sit up in bed so she will go away, and try to blink the sleep from my eyes.

"Did you have a good time last night?" Merry asks Mom, to stop the singing.

Last night. The room suddenly comes into focus with a thump of dread.

Mom's face freezes.

Cory told. I can see her doing it. I can see the way her mouth stretches down toward her chin when she tries not to cry. Of course she told. It was too big a nightmare for her skinny little body to hold.

"We did, until we got home," Mom says. "Jude, how could you?"

I can't breathe.

"I have never seen such a mess," Mom says. "Every pan and bowl in the house! You're lucky your father talked me out of waking you up and putting you to work. You're on dish duty for the week, and I don't want to hear a word about it."

I can breathe again—Cory didn't tell!—but guilt gushes through my veins. I have to tell Mom. I have to get the ashes of the bad thing I did to my sister out of my mouth and brain.

"About last night," I start.

She puts up a hand to stop me. "I know Cory had a good time with you, and I'm grateful," she says. "But these grand gestures of yours make a lot of work for everyone else."

"I know," I say. "I am so sorry. But I need to tell—"

"Not now, hon," she says, not listening. "We can talk about it later if you want to. But you've got to get ready now. Shower's free."

I am not going to think about anything but the warm needles of water scrubbing me clean. I pour shampoo into my hand and try to wash away last night, try to scour out the look on Cory's face and the sight of the shaggy young man and the girl he carried like a block of wood. I wash and wash, but the stain is still there. I realize that I am humming "I'm going to wash that man right out of my hair." I start to laugh. Then I realize there is no one who will understand how exquisitely funny this is, and I begin to laugh harder, until I am crying and the shampoo is in my eyes and Merry is pounding on the door and I have to pull myself together.

Mom has made blueberry muffins for breakfast because Dad loves them, but I'm not hungry. I give mine to Cory.

The front buzzer sounds. We all jump.

"Who's that?" I say.

Mom buzzes the front door open from the other room. I hear footsteps getting louder and louder on the stairs outside the door. Someone is breathing heavily. We hear a key go into the lock.

"Is it the StB?" Cory whispers.

"Don't be ridiculous," Mom says, and opens the door.

The figure puffing gently in our doorway is definitely *not* StB. She's a short, plump, attractive Czech woman in her fifties who beams at us before she bends over creakily to take off her shoes.

"This is Mrs. Svobodová," Mom says as the lady reaches into the hall closet for an apron and house slippers.

"Welcome, dear children," Mrs. Svobodová says, sliding into the slippers and tying the apron around her firmly corseted middle. "You are come at last. Last week it is impossible that I come. But I am great admirer of your so lovely mother, and I wish now to welcome you to the Czech lands." She solemnly shakes hands with each of us.

"At the suggestion of our hosts, I have employed Mrs. Svobodová to help us with our cooking and cleaning," Mom says.

Our hosts? We look at each other, and then figure it out. The government wants her here to keep an eye on us.

"Housekeeping can be difficult in Prague," Mrs. Svobodová says. "I am here to make it easier."

Without ado, she goes into the kitchen and begins to straighten up. I look at her padding around in her canvas slippers. I think I should feel a sense of menace, but I don't.

• • •

We take the bus to school. It turns out that we get on at the first stop of the route, so there will always be a bus ready and waiting, with plenty of seats.

I sit down next to Cory. I want to tell her that I am sorry, that I am trying to wash away last night, but she gets up and sits next to Dad. I don't blame her. I lean my forehead against the smeary, scratched bus window and close my eyes so that I don't have to see my reflection.

When I open them again, Merry is sitting next to me. "Aren't you excited?" she says, bouncing a little. "I love the first day of school!"

I smile, remembering this about her. I think about our first day at Thatcher. We were in third grade, and our stiff uniforms smelled like new books. On the way to school, we each had to hold on to one of Dad's hands at the corners because we were living in the city now and it was important not to get lost or run over. When the light turned green, we yelled, "Green means go!" and ran as fast as we could to the other side.

Merry and I were in different classrooms, but it didn't matter, because when I was really sad I would sit by the door of my room and listen, and if I concentrated hard enough I could hear Merry's voice in the next room. Or I'd catch a glimpse of her in the gym or the library, and for that moment school would be familiar and safe.

"I'm glad you're finally getting to ride the bus," she says.

I had forgotten about wanting to take the bus until she reminds me. I'd always been fiercely jealous of our classmates at Thatcher who got brightly colored bus passes from a special box every month. Lexy complained about the bus all the time, but I thought it must be nice, kind of like a little cushion between the different parts of the day.

I love Merry for remembering, for giving me back a piece of myself that I had forgotten. "Me, too," I say, and then both of us, at the same time, pump our arms for victory.

We didn't plan it. Our arms just know how to do things together. The two of us are strong in this world.

School is not right.

When we go inside, we have to take off our shoes and change into slippers. The slippers are comfortable, and if there aren't any teachers looking you can go sliding around the old wooden floors, but it's still not right.

Little kids are everywhere, like ants at a picnic. They were at Thatcher, too, but they had their own areas of the building. Here, we're all mixed in together, and the kids expect things they shouldn't. I'm just a student like them. But they give me their shoes to tie or ask me to push them on the swing at recess or open their milk cartons at lunch.

Ahmed asks us, "Are you guys balls or books?" and sniggers at the expressions on our faces.

"He means," says Freeman, "do you play soccer or study during lunch? He and Abebi always play. Sunil and I play if it's sunny, but study when we have a test coming up."

"Soccer," I say.

"Read," Merry says.

"Are you any good?" Ahmed asks me.

"She's really good," Merry says.

"How about you?" he asks her.

"She's pretty bad," I say. Merry actually likes it when I tell people the truth; if she says it, people think she's just being modest. Now they'll leave her alone about it.

Our classmates are okay. The teachers are fine. But the jelly is back, the clear jelly that muffles things and keeps me separate.

"What teams do you guys have?" I ask Abebi. We are passing a soccer ball back and forth on the front lawn while she waits for her Benz to pick her up after school. She has a great touch.

She stops the ball with her foot, taps it in the air, and catches it. Her skin is the color of polished mahogany, but the palms of her hands and her mouth are pink. The mahogany and the pink together are nice, steady colors. You can trust someone who has deep, true colors like that.

"Teams? Don't make me laugh. You think a school our size can have teams?"

Her little cousin Bem jumps on her from behind, and she laughs as she staggers backward. A horn blasts. It's the Nigerian Benz. Abebi waves at me, grabs her backpack, and walks away with her arm slung around Bem while he tells her about his day.

When I get home, I lie on my bed and concentrate on making the time go by.

BLACK LIGHT

Friday is Sunil's birthday. He invites all seven of
the kids in the class to dinner at his house and then to a black-
light theater for a play after. I don't want to go. Being polite
to parents over some disgusting spicy yogurt glop, followed
by two hours of people rolling their *r*'s in a completely incom-
prehensible language, isn't my idea of a good time.

"No, honey, it's not like that," Mom says, serving up leftover lasagna Thursday night. "The language won't matter."

"What do you mean, the language won't matter?"

"Black-light theater is not about language. It's about
images. They do all these crazy things with fluorescent lights
and neon paint and puppets and stuff. You'll love it."

"I will not. I outgrew puppet shows before I was Cory's
age."

"It's not like that," she says again. "Wait and see. You'll
have a great time."

"Yeah, well, Mrs. Montgomery will probably give us all
this gross Indian food that I've never seen before."

Mom tsks impatiently. "You sound like a spoiled Thatcher girl, Jude. Hand that plate to Cory, Mer, would you? Aside from the fact that I happen to love Indian food, I really can't see why it matters what Mrs. Montgomery makes for dinner. I think it's very gracious of her to go to the trouble of cooking for all of you. This is about Sunil and what *he* likes, anyway."

"It's not as if they can take us out to eat," Merry points out, which is true. Czech restaurants get paid the same amount by the government whether they have customers or not, so they tell you they're full even when no one's there. Plus the food is disgusting, nothing but gristle and sauerkraut and dumplings that weigh a ton, and maybe a couple of spoonfuls of mushy canned vegetables.

I try Dad. "Dad, I really don't want to go," I say.

He doesn't even look up from his dinner. "Jude, your mother has already given you her decision, and that's final."

The Montgomerys live in a villa a few streets from us on a bluff overlooking the castle and Saint Vitus Cathedral. Everything is expensive and shimmery and in its place. Mr. Montgomery is distinguished, well-dressed, and witty. Mrs. Montgomery is beautiful and welcoming, and dinner is, as Mom thought it would be, delicious.

We are in the realm of what Merry and I call the Perfect People. Thatcher was full of them. Power couples with two perfect children, a boy and a girl, and golden lives. Except usually, once you got to know them, their lives were not so golden. It turned out that the dads were never home, the moms felt trapped, the kids had issues, and everyone drank way too much.

I wait for the flaws to show themselves as we circulate around the living room, helping ourselves to exotic curries and relishes. I keep an ear out for cutting remarks from Mrs. Montgomery, skillful belittlings from Mr. Montgomery. I watch Kate and Sunil, looking for irony and angst.

Nothing.

I poke around a little bit, exploring. "You have a lovely home," I tell Mrs. Montgomery when she offers me a platter of hot, homemade *naan*.

"Thank you," she says in her beautiful South Asian voice. "We are very fortunate in having the resources to make it that way."

"It must take a lot of time to keep it up," I say.

"It does," she agrees, smiling at me. "But again, I am fortunate in that I enjoy the homemaking arts."

"Have you ever thought about doing it professionally?" I ask. This is where she won't be able to resist making allusions to the way she martyrs herself for her husband's career and her ungrateful children.

"No," she says. "I confess I am both too lazy and too picky to wish to work for someone else. The nice thing is that we are reassigned every three years, so there is always a new challenge coming."

"You don't mind all the moving?" I say.

"Well, if I had done, I would have been foolish to marry a diplomat," she says, her words cascading like notes of music. "What about you? Has this been a difficult move for you?"

Her words surprise me. No one has asked me that before. Without warning, I feel stinging in my eyes and behind my nose. I stare at her, fumbling for something to say that will cover me up. But her eyes are kind, and I cannot lie to kindness.

"It's been awful," I say. "I hate it. I want to go home."

With a quick, flowing movement she puts her platter down on a carved wooden sideboard and hugs me. "Oh, my dear, I am so sorry," she says.

The bones of her shoulder are as small and light as a bird's wing. I hold myself slightly away from her, worried that the salt that stings my eyes will stain the fragile silk of her apricot-colored sari. She smells, unexpectedly, of Chanel No. 5, my grandmother's perfume.

She lets me go, and I see that her face is as gentle and serene as a Michelangelo Madonna. "Of course you are unhappy," she says, her voice warm with sympathy. "You are sixteen years old—"

"Fifteen," I say.

"Fifteen years old, and just beginning to grow into yourself. You have no time or energy to spare for all the confusion and compromise of a new culture. This must be a very difficult time for you."

"That's it," I say, barely able to form the words. "That's exactly how I feel."

"Of course it is," she says. "Nothing is more natural. So tell me, Judith. What are some of the things you do to make your heart strong?"

Her words come too quickly while I am still noticing how

open and calm she has made me. I repeat them so that their flavor will spread through my mind. "My heart strong? Do you mean how do I make myself feel better?"

"Not exactly," she says slowly. She looks around and finds a seat on a brocade loveseat, patting the cushion next to her for me to join her. "Making yourself feel better is not always the same as making your heart strong." She frowns absently at the skirt of her sari, pleating it a little in her fingers. Her face clears. "Ah. This is the difference. When I am sad, ice cream nearly always makes me feel better. But it doesn't heal the sadness. It just pushes it away for a little. Once the ice cream is gone, the sadness comes back—and it's usually worse because I have fallen off my diet.

"What I mean by making your heart strong is the kind of thing you do that does more than make you forget the sad thing for a minute. It's the kind of thing that makes you less vulnerable to the sadness in the first place." She looks at me to see if I understand, but I guess I don't look like I do, because she keeps talking, and now it's with the "Once upon a time" kind of sound.

"Every fall as the days get shorter, I find myself falling into a little depression. Sometime in November, or it may be October, there comes a day when I am overwhelmed by all the gray. Not only in Prague, but anywhere at all that is not home. My body craves the sun and heat so strongly that I think there must be a chemical reason for the way I feel.

"For years I made myself miserable by getting out pictures of home and looking at travel guides and trying to imagine myself in the place I wanted so badly to be. And for just a moment here or there, it was almost enough. I could almost taste my mother's cooking. I could almost smell the wind on the beach. Almost. But never quite. And the more I thought about it, the farther away it seemed." She is looking at a small photograph on a table next to me, of a large house set in bright fields edged with palm trees.

"Finally, one day—we were in Ottawa; Sunil must have been two or three—I had taken him to the park and began thinking of home and started to cry. Sunil came over and climbed up on my lap and said, 'Momma, why does your face always look so sad?'

"Without even thinking about it, I said, 'Because my bones miss the fire of the sun.'"

She laughs and shakes her head. "He had no idea what I was talking about, of course. But about a week later we were at some function where they served Baked Alaska, and you know how they stick sparklers in it?"

I nod.

"Sunil was a solemn little boy," she says. "He didn't talk much, especially not in company. But when he saw the sparklers his eyes got very big and he stood very still and then he said, 'Momma! Here's some fire from the sun!'"

I glance over to where Sunil is sitting talking with Freeman and Merry. I can see the little boy inside his tall body, and the way his big brown eyes would have caught the light and reflected it back again.

"It may have been silly, but I asked the maitre d' for some sparklers, and that night after we got home I lit them and pretended that they were the sun. But they weren't hot enough.

So I combed through all the cabinets in the house and gathered up every candle I could find and lined them up on the bathroom cabinet and lit them all. Every single one. There must have been two dozen of them, plus a box of birthday candles I stuck in a loaf of bread, all lined up in front of the mirror so that when I lit them it looked like a field of candles. I put my hands as close to the flames as I could and held them there until the heat became uncomfortable, and then I blew them out."

"You blew the candles *out?*" The words startle from my mouth. "Why?"

"So I could light them again," she says. "I went through the whole process about a dozen times, until I had convinced myself that I could make as much light and heat as I wanted whenever I wanted to—I could spend the rest of my life lighting fires if that's what I wanted to do. And that was enough. So this time of year, when I begin to get blue, I light a candle. And if it's been a really bad day, I light two. Or three."

She puts her finger to her lips and lifts up the corner of the embroidered cloth arranged over the table at my side. I see that the table is actually a wine safe, with a door in the front that opens. She pulls it open far enough for me to see what she keeps inside. Candles. Boxes and boxes of candles.

She closes the door, softly, lovingly, and smooths the tablecloth back into place. "So again I ask, what are the things you do that make you strong, so that you are ready to bear what must be borne? What are your candles?"

"I don't know," I say. "It's mostly been sports before. But Abebi says ISC is too small for teams."

"You are an athlete, are you?" Mrs. Montgomery says. "What are your sports?"

"Soccer and hockey mostly. A little basketball and softball."

She claps her hands and the bangles on her slender arms jangle. "Hockey? And soccer? You have come to the right place." She looks around the room, her eyes settling on the couches where Kate, Abebi, Sophy, and Ahmed are chatting. "Come with me," she says, taking my arm with her soft brown fingers and leading me over to the little group.

"I am so sorry to interrupt," she says, breaking into their conversation. "But this is news that cannot wait. Judith plays hockey."

"No kidding!" says Kate, her face brightening. "Are you any good?"

"I'm okay," I say. "Do you play?"

She rolls her eyes. "I'm half-Canadian. What do you think? Sunil and Ahmed, too. We play pretty much every Saturday morning once the rinks open."

I feel my face splitting into one huge grin. "Really? You want another player?"

Kate looks over at Sunil.

"Tomorrow morning, eleven o'clock, rain or shine, Letná Park," he says, and I can see the candles shining in his eyes.

Tomorrow I am playing hockey. Tomorrow I am playing hockey. I can't keep a stupid grin off my face. We go to the theater, and fish and teapots fly through the air, neon ultraviolet lights dancing on invisible backs and shoulders wrapped in black velvet. It's fast and fun and silly, like *Fantasia* on speed, and Mom was right, the language doesn't matter. When it is over, I clap and clap and clap to say thank you, *thank you,* to the actors who have painted themselves in such bright lights.

THE **HARVEST**

Sunday morning at breakfast, Mom and Dad tell us to put on our church clothes. Cory and I choke on our waffles.

"I thought you decided the branch in Nuremberg was too far away," I say.

"We did," Dad says. "Especially since by the terms of her fellowship, your mother is not supposed to leave the country until the school year is over."

"Then why does she go get groceries in Germany every Wednesday?" Cory asks.

Mom looks uncomfortable. "I probably shouldn't," she admits. "But it was the DCM's wife who asked me to go with them, so I figure this is one of those things where they look the other way because the food here isn't very healthy."

"Plus that's really the only time Mom gets to talk to anyone besides us," Merry points out. "She's in the library the rest of the time."

"So why do we have to wear church clothes if we're not going to church?" Cory asks.

"As a sign of respect for the Lord's Day," Dad says.

"That's stupid," Cory says.

"It's better than schlepping out to Nuremberg every week, believe you me," mutters Merry. "Don't push it."

"Tell you what," Dad says, giving Mom a significant look. "Mom and I thought going to a classical music concert like the one we heard last week at the castle might be a good substitute for church. As long as you guys are good sports about getting dressed up and going to a concert with us every Sunday, you can wear whatever you want for the rest of the day."

"How long are the concerts?" Cory wants to know.

"Less than two hours," Mom says.

"Two *hours*?"

"Hey, at least it's shorter than driving to Nuremberg," Merry says. "I'm game."

Cory and I look at each other. "Okay," I say, grudgingly.

But when we get outside an hour later, Mom and Dad turn away from the castle and toward Leninová instead.

"Dad, the castle's that way," I say.

He and Mom look around, then motion us to all scrunch up close next to them under a big linden tree.

"What?" I say.

"There's a church here in Prague," Dad says.

I look at him like he has lost his mind. "No duh," I say. "There are probably a million churches."

"No," Dad says. "A Mormon church."

"There is?" Merry says, completely shocked. "Here? How come no one has said anything?"

"Communists think religion is a bunch of made-up nonsense that rich people use to get the poor to behave," Dad says. "The Mormons here have to be very careful. The police will haul them in for questioning at the drop of a hat, so we have to be discreet. Now, the service is a little shorter here than it was at home—somewhere around an hour and a half, two hours. It's held in the bishop's living room, so when we get to the building it's important not to make a lot of noise or draw attention to yourself in any way. They don't want the neighbors to get suspicious."

"We've decided that we'll go every other week," Mom says. "That way we're only half as likely to draw attention to the group. We won't stay for Sunday school, since you won't understand the Czech, but at least we can sing a hymn and take the sacrament. We can't use the car, because the police know our license plate, but they're not following us or anything, so it should be okay if we take the metro."

We get on the metro at Leninová, but Mom and Cory get off a stop before we do so that we arrive at different times and from different directions.

We go to an ordinary apartment building. The door clicks open as soon as we ring the buzzer. I look around as we walk inside, and see a hand pulling back a lace curtain in a window across the street. Someone is watching.

Mom and Cory are already there when we get upstairs to the apartment. We walk into a shabby living room crowded with three old couches, a bunch of chairs, and a dining room table covered with a white cloth that I guess they're using as the sacrament table. The blinds are down and the windows are closed, and it's so quiet that you can hear everyone breathing. There aren't many people—maybe eight or ten, all with that faded, slippery, don't-look-at-me invisibleness that everyone wears in Prague. And they're old. During the hymn, "Gently Raise the Sacred Strain," which they sing in Czech but we sing in English, raising it so gently we are practically whispering, I try to imagine what it would be like to come to a room like this one for forty years, knowing every time you did that a neighbor might get suspicious or the person next to you might be an informant.

It's hard to sit still in this room that smells of coal smoke and bread and sour cabbage and listen to words I don't understand. And it's empty. Church has always felt like a warm, safe nest. But I don't feel safe here. I don't know these people's stories, and they don't know mine. I look at them, at their strange, poor clothes and blank faces, and I want to go home.

The blankness of those faces creeps under my skin. I stare out the window at school, trying to find my way back to before the faces. But all I can see is the emptiness. It's better at home because my bed is a nest. I pull the covers over my head and try to remember something that will make my heart strong. But it's too much work.

On Wednesday Sunil comes home with us to study for the history test. He sits at my desk with his long legs and his long arms and there is too much of him. I take my book and go into the living room.

Prague's thick afternoon light streams in the windows, touching all the empty space with gold so that I cannot forget it is there. I feel my flesh dissolving into all the emptiness, so I find a nest in the corner, behind the couch. The burr of Mrs. Svobodová's vacuum wanders down the hall from Cory's room and wraps itself around me.

I might be asleep. Then my name drops through the air like a stone, and I am awake. "Your girl Jude, she is not happy," I hear Mrs. Svobodová say from the kitchen.

Some water turns off.

"I know," I hear my mother say. She sighs, and I imagine that I can feel her breath blowing into my face. "We are worried about her."

They are? Anger licks at my throat. If they're so concerned about me, why don't they fix things?

"May I offer you some lemonade?" Mom says, sounding fake. Chairs clatter across the kitchen tile, and my anger grows, chasing the emptiness away.

"I would be pleased," Mrs. Svobodová says. "Mrs. Virginia, I see the picture in the silver frame."

I look at the picture that stands on the end table next to the couch. Nana took it of Grandpop teaching me and Merry how to prune. I remember that day. I remember the hot smell of the grapes and the way the vines jabbed at my wrists.

"Your girls, do they work with the vines?"

Ice clinks in a glass. "Yes," Mom says, sounding—surprised? Suspicious? "My parents own a vineyard. The girls used to go up and help on the weekends and in the summer."

"I think so," says Mrs. Svobodová. "The girls also, they say things that make me think this is so. Thank you, dear lady."

I hear ice clanking and drinking noises.

"I have talked to my man," Mrs. Svobodová continues. "This weekend, he goes home to Mikulov to help his sister tend the vines. You know Mikulov? It is in Moravia, near to the Austrian border. It is a good place, in the country, where the air is fresh."

My mother doesn't answer. After a minute, Mrs. Svobodová clicks her tongue impatiently. "Mrs. Virginia, I am making you an invitation. Your daughters would be welcome in my sister-in-law's house."

Is that even legal? For an American to stay at a Czech person's home?

"Mrs. Svobodová—Marcela—that is an incredibly generous offer," my mother begins. "But we would not want to put you in a difficult position."

"Is no difficult position," she says. "It is in the country. No one cares about the country. Besides, I am thinking that your Judith, she is missing the vines. My man, he knows what it is to miss the vines. So."

I hear the chair going back, and Mrs. Svobodová getting to her feet. "He departs after work on Thursday. I think Friday there is no school for the girls because the parents come to see the teachers, yes? So there should be no problem. He will wait until the girls come home. They can be ready, yes?"

"I suppose so," says Mom, sounding dazed. "You're sure this won't make trouble for you?"

"Mrs. Virginia, I am Czech. We Czechs do not like trouble. I am not asking if there is trouble. Now, I leave a little early. There are preparations I must make."

"Of course," Mom says, like she would do anything Mrs. Svobodová asks.

Mr. Svoboda picks us up at three o'clock sharp in his taxi, a tiny, noisy tin can of a car, stinking of diesel and wet cigarettes. We haven't brought much—a backpack each—which is good, because the trunk is full of ancient metal gas cans.

"You see this gasoline?" he asks us. "She is the best gasoline in Prague." He puts his finger next to his nose and says, "I have a friend." Then he winks. "I must be good to my car." And just as carefully as if his rattly old Škoda were a Rolls-Royce, he closes the trunk, holds the back door open for us, and then closes it and hops into his seat.

And then hops out again, after opening the glove compartment and extracting a bottle of cleaning liquid and an old rubber squeegee wrapped in a dirty handkerchief. He cleans the back window, the side windows, the front window, and the side mirrors with quick, practiced strokes of the squeegee, which leaves a line of liquid behind where the rubber blade is nicked; wraps it back in the handkerchief; and replaces it tenderly in the glove compartment. This is more complicated than it sounds, since the knob for the glove compartment is gone and he has to fiddle around to get it to open. Then, even though it is about a hundred degrees out, he pulls on a pair of ancient driving gloves, and, sitting very straight, starts the car, checks his blind spots, and lets out the clutch.

The Škoda doesn't have air conditioning, of course, which means that we spend the first few minutes of the trip wrestling our windows open (Merry's needs a good tug from the top). Four open windows make any kind of conversation between Mr. Svoboda in the front seat and us in the back pretty much impossible, which is a bonus. I lean my head against the sticky vinyl and pretend we are on our way to Meadowbrook in Grandpop's jeep.

We bob up and down gentle hills that strain the Škoda's engine almost to a stall as we make our way across Bohemia. Twice we stop to help a broken-down car even more pathetic than our own. One of them is a Trabant. When we get back in the car, Mr. Svoboda wipes his hands and shakes his head.

"Those East German cars, they are garbage," he says. "Do you know what they are made of? Plastic and pieces of old carpets."

"Fiberglass," Merry says.

"Yes. Fiberglass," he says. He pats the cracked vinyl dashboard. "We Czechs would never make cars like that." He puts the key in the ignition, throws his head back, and bursts into song. An old Beatles standard, the kind that can get you reported to the StB if you forget and hum it on the subway.

A smile stretches my lips as the engine wheezes to life. A minute later, Merry catches my eye, and I can't stop myself from smiling even more. It is the two of us taking on the world the way it has always been as we chug along toward the Svobodas' vineyard in the golden afternoon light, singing Beatles songs with Mr. Svoboda at the top of our lungs.

When we get to Brno, the capital of the eastern Czech region of Moravia, Mr. Svoboda drives right into the city center, turns in to a parking space the size of a toaster, and kills the motor. "It is Thursday," he announces. "So I buy some books for my sister."

"Thursday is the day that new books come out in Czechoslovakia," Merry says in a bossy, self-important way as we unfold ourselves from the second seat. "Sunil told me. It's the social event of the week. They list the titles in the newspaper and everything."

"No duh," I say, and when she crosses the square to wait for Mr. Svoboda outside the bookstore, I let her go.

I look around the large, bare square. It must have been beautiful once. Big, solid stone buildings designed to look like Renaissance palaces and Gothic cathedrals stand guard over it, but their graceful lines are obscured by the droop of the tram wires that web the streets, and their plaster walls are cracked and faded. A huge Plague Column erected to thank God for ending an epidemic of the Black Death stands in the center. It's a relic of the Catholic faith, so it should have been torn down, but apparently some party functionary couldn't be bothered. I can't tear my eyes away from it. Distorted, soot-blackened saints and cherubs swarm over its surface like a colony of ants on a giant anthill. Something cold and small skitters across the inside of my chest. When there's a break in the traffic, I cross the square and join Merry.

She's leaning against a tree, watching the pantomime slowly playing out behind the dusty plate-glass window of the bookstore. A woman in a tight cotton dress and a scarf covering her hair approaches the cash desk. She and the cashier greet each other. The customer asks for a book. The cashier shakes her head. The customer pulls out a newspaper and shows her the announcement the store has published. The cashier shrugs. The customer waits while the clerk walks to the locked display window, unlocks it, retrieves the book, relocks the case, returns to the counter, rings the purchase up, and writes out a receipt. The cashier wraps the book and ties it with string. They shake hands and say their goodbyes. Then a little man in cheap sneakers sidles up to the counter, and the whole thing begins all over again.

I watch, the anxious feeling of the swarming saints slowly smoothed and soothed away by the slow, repetitive dance between the clerk and the long line of customers. I daydream, imagining the little man taking his book home and unwrapping it tenderly, being careful not to tear the paper so it can be used again, settling in for an evening with his new book, reading it slowly so that it lasts, savoring each precious word.

"I have them!" a voice says loudly.

I jump.

It's Mr. Svoboda, looking pleased with himself and brandishing a package wrapped in newspaper. "I have four! Four books! Anežka will be very happy with me."

We follow him to the Škoda and wait while he unlocks the trunk, nestles the books in an old blanket, and extracts a can of fuel and a funnel. He fills the tank, wipes off the can carefully with a rag he apparently keeps for that very purpose, and puts it back into the trunk. Then, instead of unlocking the car doors for us as I expect him to, he rubs his hands together with a pleased expression on his face. "That is done," he says. "Now I wish you to join me for some refreshment."

I assume he means a glass of *pivo,* and, thinking of all the gas in the trunk, follow him a little unwillingly down a side street to a heavy oak door. But when he tugs it open, we are greeted by the heavy, fatty smell of roasted meat and bread dumplings. We are in an old wine cellar—complete with barrel-vaulted brick walls, communal tables, and benches of thick oak—that has been converted to a restaurant. Smoke from three dozen cheap cigarettes makes my eyes sting before we are all the way inside. But the service is pretty good by Czechoslovakian standards, and a few minutes later we are tucking into goulash and bread dumplings.

No one says much during the meal. By the time the waitress brings sweet cheese dumplings for us and coffee for Mr. Svoboda, I figure it's time to break the silence. I look around at the dark, dusty room, searching for something to say. "How old is this place, anyway?" I say.

"Not so old," Mr. Svoboda says, stirring sugar into his coffee. "Maybe two hundred, three hundred years. My sister Anežka and I eat here when she taught at the university."

"And this is the same sister whose house we're staying at."

"Yeah. She was a professor of English. Is how I learn my English."

"She is retired?" Czech women retire in their mid-fifties, depending on how many children they have.

"Yeah, she is retired," he says. "But before that she is not teaching at the university for many years." He signals for the check. "She was a teacher at a nursery school in Mikulov."

The waitress brings a slip of paper.

"Mr. Svoboda," I say, "it would be our honor to—"

He looks at me over his heavy reading glasses, surprised, and suppresses a smile as he realizes what I am trying to do. "Mrs. Virginia, she give me money," he says. "For the gasoline, too. You do not worry." He looks down at the paper and his bottom lip juts out as he checks the figures, takes out his wallet, and lays some notes on the dish that had come with the bill. Then he glances at his watch and whips off his glasses. "You wish to use the toilet?" he asks.

Mr. Svoboda's sister is waiting for us by the front door as we pull up, a smaller, paler version of her brother, with gray hair pulled back from an unlined face and eyes the color of grape hyacinths. She is wearing a cheap cotton dress and an apron and canvas slippers, the uniform of a Czechoslovakian housewife, and the hand she puts out for us to shake is callused and businesslike with short, clean nails, but when she says, "Welcome, dear friends," her voice is as soft and rich as a cashmere scarf.

"Anežka," says Mr. Svoboda, taking her hands and kissing her on both cheeks. "Marcela sends her love."

"You are looking fit," Miss Svobodová responds in excellent English. "Have you eaten?"

"Yes. We stopped in Brno."

"Good," she says. "I thought you might, so I have only a cold supper. Which one is Meredith and which one Judith? Yes, I see. Please call me Anežka. Come. I will show you the house."

Anežka's house is a study in contrasts. It is tiny, not much bigger than the dirt-floored houses our history class went to see at the living history village, and set flush against the road; I imagine Austrian officials coming by on horseback and talking to the house's inhabitants through open windows without having to dismount. But although she sleeps on a pullout bed in the front room, next to the kitchen, and her bathroom is nothing but a sink and a toilet with a rusty pull chain and the tank mounted on the wall above it, you can tell there used to be money.

The front room bristles with embroidery and lace and dark, carved wood furniture designed for rooms three or four times its size. Whatnot shelves near the windows sparkle with leaded crystal in ruby, sapphire, and emerald. One dark wall is covered with black-and-white photographs of sports teams taken a half century ago. I look more closely. In one shot I recognize a younger, thinner Anežka proudly holding her team's volleyball; in another, she's participating in some kind of huge parade.

"What was that for?" Merry asks.

"Sokol. Do you know it?"

We shake our heads.

"It's a big organization for physical and mental fitness, like your Boy Scouts or Girl Scouts, I think. Except it is for Czechs of all ages. My husband also. He was a very fine football player." She runs a finger along a large photograph of a soccer team, stopping on a tall, rangy, dark-haired man. "Yes. This is he. Dušan."

"Jude plays soccer, too," Merry offers. "She's really good."

Anežka smiles at me. "I am glad to hear it. In fact, I am

officiating at a game Saturday afternoon. You must come and see how we Czechs play."

"That would be great," I say.

She doesn't say anything else about her husband, nor is there any sign of him in the house besides the photographs, so I decide that he must have died.

Mr. and Mrs. Svoboda's apartment is upstairs. It, too, is simple: a living room furnished with a huge horsehair couch, three chairs, a massive desk, two lamps, and lots of bookshelves; and a bedroom with more bookshelves and a bed piled high with pillows. Their kitchen is a tiny stove with a battered frying pan and a teakettle tucked into an alcove at the top of the stairs; it is powered by a tank of propane propped on a jerry-rigged platform outside the small window that lights the staircase. Their bathroom is a jug of water and a washbasin on a stand.

We unpack and wash our hands and faces, then go downstairs, where Anežka and Mr. Svoboda—Josef—are waiting. "So," Josef says. "You wish to see the vines?"

"Josef, it is late. That can wait until tomorrow," Anežka says.

"Nonsense," he says. "The little ones miss the vines. We will go tonight."

The village of Bavory rings a small park dotted with clumps of trees. But Josef leads us away from the center of town, smudged now with the blue shadows of evening and edged with the lacy fingers of the birch trees, and up into limestone hills that are pale under the full moon. And here at last are the vines.

No one says much. We walk up and down the rows of heavy translucent grapes sweetening on the vine. A few of the rows have been given over at one end to vegetables—tomatoes, squash, carrots, maybe peas and beans earlier in the season. It isn't a large vineyard—just one hectare, about two and a half acres. But it's big enough to feel like home. I strip off a grape and crush it with my teeth, then suck on it for a moment. The sugar is about there. I pinch off one of the big leaves of the canopy and brush the tiny hairs on its top against my cheek before I roll it between my fingers. Its sharp green earthiness stains my hands.

I look up to see Anežka watching me. Her eyes are black pools in the darkness. "It is always good to come back to the vines," she says.

I look away so she won't see that her kindness makes me cry.

By two o'clock the next day, I am tired and my back hurts. I stretch backward, my arms at my waist, and circle around, trying to ease some of the stiffness, and catch Anežka doing the same. "You two are good workers," she says. "I think someone has trained you well. But now it is time for a break. Can you ride bicycles? And, more important, did you bring your swimsuits?"

Actually, we did. We always do when we go away—a bathing suit doesn't take up much room and you never know when it will come in handy.

The bikes are old and rusty, so we grease the chains and hope for the best. Wearing nothing but bathing suits and sandals, we wobble behind Anežka's erect figure down a succession of country lanes, planted on either side with sour cherry trees whose trunks are painted white. The cherries are past, but Anežka says they are beautiful in the spring.

We eventually come to a swampy sort of lake with a small rickety pier built out at one end. Although Merry is usually squeamish about fish and snapping turtles, we are all so hot and dusty that she drops her bike, kicks off her sandals, and dives into the murky water as quickly as I do.

The water is cool and thick against my skin. I surface, breathing in the familiar green scent of pond and growing things, and look around for the others while I tread water. Merry is picking off some lake grass that got caught in her hair. Beyond her, I see Anežka running the length of the pier in her old, belted bathing suit, her big and beautiful arms pumping. She dives into the lake and then surfaces between us, shooting water between her front teeth like an especially powerful mermaid posing for a fountain.

"Welcome," she says in her cashmere voice, "to Moravia." Then one arm goes around my waist and the other under my feet, and I am airborne, suspended above the lake while water droplets fall like jewels from my feet.

The next afternoon, the whole village of Bavory packs up and goes to Saturday-night soccer in Mikulov, a kilometer away. Josef, who is wrestling with a broken pipe, tells Anežka to take us early so we can see the castle. She is not happy about this, but when we say it is not necessary, she tells us that it is and to bring our cameras, there is a view.

Mikulov was the center of Moravian Jewry. Before the war, there were five synagogues here. Now there is only one, and it is a museum. The Jews are long gone, dead at Auschwitz or Terezín. Our class has visited most of the Jewish sites in and around Prague. They are heavy, sad places where the ghosts of grief suck at you like quicksand, but the synagogue in Mikulov is not. I don't know why.

We climb up to the castle, which protected the king's Jewish bankers and artisans from angry Christian peasants. We walk inside a big iron gate that Merry says reminds her of *The Sound of Music* to find large, graceful trees and a soft green lawn that floods up to a stone wall, just like the soccer field at home.

The wall overlooks a broad plain that stretches to the horizon, dotted here and there with clusters of cottages and lent texture by the various greens of vines, fields, and orchards. We are too far away to see anything but its beauty; I feel as though we are looking at an idealized, department-store-window version of village life in Central Europe. It is too perfect to be real, except for an ugly dark gash about halfway between us and the horizon.

"What *is* that?" I ask Merry. "A road or something?"

"Too narrow and no cars," she says.

"A narrow-gauge railroad?"

"How would I know?" she says, irritated. Merry doesn't like not knowing the answer. "Ask Anežka."

I look around and find her sitting on a bench with her back to the view.

"Anežka, what is that black thing across the field?" I call.

Anežka doesn't move for a minute, and I think she hasn't heard us. Then she stands up very straight and comes slowly toward us. "That is the Austrian border," she says.

We look again, and now that I know what I am looking at I can make out barbed wire and soldiers stationed at regular intervals.

"It's so near," Merry says. "You could almost throw a stone that far."

"Yes," Anežka says, like she is closing a book. She looks at her watch. "The football will be starting," she says. "We should go."

Everyone from both villages is at the game. There are no uniforms, just shirts and skins. I think they ask me to play mostly so they can use the leather soccer ball I have brought with me. But I am better than they expected, and soon they are calling my name—"Yude! Yude!"—and passing to me.

I am sorry when we are done. I tell them that they should see me play hockey, and they invite me back when the lake is frozen.

Blood is singing in my veins. Josef slaps me on the back with his big rough hand. "Not bad for an American," he says, his eyes twinkling.

I am pleased, but before I think of something to say back to him, I see that he is frowning. At first I think it is because my words do not come quickly enough. Then I see he is looking beyond my shoulder.

A scruffy band of people with dusty, uncombed hair is emerging noisily from the woods, arms full of babies and musical instruments. Brown-skinned children with piercing voices caper around them. Josef spits. "Gypsies," he says. "You girls be careful."

I am shocked by his undisguised dislike. "Careful of what?" I say.

He looks back and forth between me and Merry. "Don't you have Gypsies in America?" he asks.

We shake our heads.

"You are lucky!" he says.

"What do you mean?" I ask coldly.

"They are nothing but thieves," he says. "I mean this literally. When it is time for them to marry, Gypsy men do not look for women who will keep a good home and be good mothers to their children. They look for women who are skilled at stealing the property of others so they will never have to work."

Anežka has come up behind us without my noticing. "What nonsense are you telling the children, Josef?" she says. "They will think you are a bigoted, narrow-minded peasant."

"Can you deny the truth of what I say?" he demands.

She purses her lips. "No, I suppose not," she admits.

"Marcela and I waited four years for an apartment before we could be married," Josef tells us. "We were very pleased when we were told we had been assigned an apartment in a new building. Unfortunately for us, our neighbors were Gypsies. Do you know the first thing they did? Tore up the wood flooring for firewood."

"Is that really true?" Merry asks skeptically.

"I swear it on my mother's grave," Josef says.

"They had never lived in a city before," Anežka tells us. She is carrying a blanket and a picnic basket, and gestures with her head to a rickety card table where an old woman is selling new wine. "Josef, my mouth tastes like dust. Would you be so kind …"

"Now my sister will apologize for my bad manners," Josef grumbles. "But if you had seen them, as I did, stuffing ten or twenty into an apartment meant for four. Breaking everything. Stealing everything. Up at all hours of the day or night, screaming and dancing and hitting and I don't know what."

"Josef. Some wine," Anežka says.

"All right, all right," he says. "But you keep a close watch on your ball, Judith. And anything else you do not wish to lose."

He stumps off for the wine while Anežka puts down her burden. Merry and I spread out the cloth, and she begins to unpack bread, grapes, cheese.

Merry stands staring at the Gypsies. I hand her some grapes and she begins to eat them absently.

"Is all that really true?" she asks Anežka.

Anežka is pouring bottled water over her hands. She reaches for a towel and begins to dry them as she answers. "Yes, I am afraid so. It is a different way of life, one that does not fit so easily with Czech ways." She slices a loaf of heavy, dark bread, holding it against her chest like a football. "My mother was the village teacher when we were small, and she used to hate it when the Gypsies came. They never stayed long, but while they were there, nothing was safe—your lunch, your pen, the ribbon in your hair. You couldn't blame the children, really. They had so little and it was their way of life. But it was hard for us to understand." She hands me the bread and gives me a mischievous grin. "I think one reason Josef is so bitter is that they always seemed to come the week after his birthday. He never managed to hold on to his gifts for very long."

The Gypsies begin to tune up their instruments. Josef comes back and distributes paper cups of grape juice. Anežka pulls a serving dish from her bag and hands it to Josef. He sighs and goes off again to stand in line for grilled bratwurst and tomatoes.

A violin begins to play, thin and sad, then another. Josef brings back the dish filled with hot, fragrant sausage and tomatoes, and we eat them with the bread and mustard until I begin to think that, like the sausage itself, I will pop out of my skin. The music swirls around us until everyone is singing, even Josef, everyone but me and Merry, because we don't know the words. But then the dancing begins and the words don't matter. I dance with a little girl whose eyes are as big and dark and shiny as the pond at Nana and Grandpop's. We dance and dance and soon the music and the night are inside me, and so are the Gypsies.

There is no work on Sunday. Anežka shows us her English books, old friends like *Jane Eyre* and *Pride and Prejudice* and *David Copperfield*. Merry and I take them outside and find a hollow place in the hill, where we sit and read and eat rye bread and tomatoes and cucumbers dressed with wine vinegar and salt. I tuck my feet under Merry's legs.

Too early, it is time to go. Anežka gives us bread and cheese for the journey, and grapes that are still warm from the sun. She hugs me tight with her powerful arms, and I breathe in the smell of the vines. "Come back soon, little one," she says. "My door is always open for you."

She stands by her door waving until we are gone.

I wake up when Mr. Svoboda turns off the ignition. We are parked in front of our apartment building. The sun is gone, but when I get out of the car I hear my name. I look up, and there's Cory waving and calling from a light-filled window. She has been waiting for us. When we get upstairs, she is wearing her soft Hanna pajamas stamped with pictures of horses and my love for her swells until I think I will burst.

FALLING

Mom is taking brownies out of the oven, brownies she made for us because she missed us. They are hot and fragrant, and she cuts them right away before they have cooled, like I always want her to but she never does, while Dad pours us glasses of icy-cold milk. Cory climbs onto my lap and puts her pink, smooth arms around me. Her neck smells of soap, and we laugh and tease Mom when the brownies fall apart because she didn't let them cool enough, and then, too soon, Cory's head is heavy on my shoulder. I start to get up to put her to bed, but Mom says not to worry, it's my first night back and she'll take care of it, and besides, there's something she wants to show Merry in the other room.

Except it turns out that's all a lie, all of it. As soon as the door shuts behind them, Dad tells me to leave the dishes, that we need to have a little talk. "Your mother and I were sobered by our conferences with your teachers on Friday," he says, shoving his glasses up his nose and getting straight to the point. "They say you're not doing your homework, and that your first set of tests were pretty much a disaster. Now, we wouldn't care what your grades were as long as you were doing your best, but you are a very bright young woman and this is clearly not your best."

He waits for me to say something, but nothing comes to mind.

Mom comes in and starts to clear the table, but Dad gestures for her to leave the dishes and take a seat. "I was just telling Jude that we were concerned about her midterm reports. Is there anything you'd like to add, Ginny?"

Mom sits down next to me and takes my hand. "Just that we're worried about you, Jude. You've always been a good student—maybe not the most diligent on record, but responsive and engaged. But that is not the person we heard your teachers describe on Friday. They said you seem to spend most of your time just sort of spaced out. One of them even asked us if we had reason to believe you might be experimenting with drugs."

I feel all the warm, good feeling seeping away, the warmth of the weekend and the brownies and Cory waiting at the window, and it makes me want to take my fingernails and rake them across my parents' faces for spoiling everything. I shrug.

"And there was your physics exam last spring," Dad presses. "You were at the top of the class all year and then didn't bother answering most of the questions on the final. We thought at the time it was a one-shot deal, but in retrospect we're not so sure. What can you tell us about that?"

My face gets hot. That physics exam was a long time ago, so long ago that I'd forgotten all about it. It's not fair of them to bring it up now. It's like they want to make sure that my mistakes follow me around forever.

"Is there something going on we should know about?" Mom asks.

"You know what's going on. I don't like Prague," I say. "I don't have any friends here. I want to go home."

"Well, that's not an option, so let's think of a realistic alternative," Mom says. "If you're missing your friends, why don't you write them?"

I shove back from the table so hard that my chair tips over backward and crashes onto the hard tile. I manage not to fall with it, but instead of being happy about that, Dad rights it and impatiently gestures for me to take it.

I give him the snotty teenage "What*ever*" look that I know he despises.

"Sit," he says. "Now."

I try to stare him down, but he's been through this too many times with too many students. No way is he going to blink.

"Fine," I say. I flop into the chair so that its wooden legs screech unpleasantly against the tile. "But what I want to know is, what happened to all that stuff about 'We don't care what your grades are as long as you are doing your best'? Just because everyone can't be perfect like Merry …"

"Spare us the crap," Dad says. "It is abundantly clear that you are not doing anywhere near your best. What we want to know is what you are prepared to do about it."

They wait while my thumb chases a bunch of brownie crumbs around an empty plate.

"Well," Dad says after a few minutes. "If you're not going to do it on your own, I guess we'll have to step in and help you. We've got a new rule. Starting tomorrow, you're to come straight home from school so you have plenty of time to do your homework while you are still fresh. Mom will make sure she's home from the library in time to supervise you."

For a moment I am afraid I will fly into pieces. Mom and Dad are doing something bad to me. They are supposed to take care of me, but they're not. They have brought me to this bad place and now they are taking away the only part of the day when I can fly.

"Is there anything you want to say?" Mom asks.

I won't look at them, afraid that if I do, I will see bad creatures peering out of my parents' eyes.

"Look, honey, we've got only two and a half more years with you," Mom says. "That may sound like a long time, but you're going to be applying to college before you know it. Your grades are simply too important to sacrifice to social activities."

I feel that last sentence like a blow. Doesn't she know I'm not doing this on purpose? That she doesn't know, that no one knows, that I am truly alone—the fear strikes me like a bolt of lightning, shocking me from the inside out, sending electrons spinning in ways they are not supposed to go. And it gets bigger and bigger, pressing against me until there is no more room, until my skin parts, as it did once before, but this time it is worse, because it is tearing from the inside. "*Why* are you *doing* this?" I cry.

"Because we love you," Mom says like she's reminding me not to forget my backpack. "And we want the best for you."

"That's *bogus*! *You're* bogus! I *hate* you!" I shriek. I don't know what to do. I want to shred my clothes or pull out my hair. I take the empty plate and hurl it against the tile floor, where it shatters.

Everything stops, but the fear is still growing. Sobbing, I scrabble for the pieces so I can throw them again and again.

"Jude! Stop! You'll cut yourself, you young idiot," Dad says, grabbing for my arm.

I press my thumb ever so lightly against the sharp edge of one of the splinters. No one can see. It's only me who can feel it. *Pop!* The cells part like the casing of a sausage and a thin line of crimson oozes from my thumb, then thickens to a stream. I open my hand and let the pieces of the plate fall. Mom and Dad exclaim and search for bandages and anti-septic, but their voices and actions cannot touch me. I am still at last.

"Quite a weekend, huh, guys," Freeman greets us as we change into slippers the next morning at school.

"Yeah, it turned out better than I thought it would," Merry says.

Freeman looks confused. "What are you talking about?"

"Our visit to Bavory," Merry says. "What are *you* talking about?"

"The East Germans," he says, like we're supposed to know already.

But this time Merry doesn't know either. "The who?"

"The East Germans."

Merry and I look at each other blankly.

"You guys knew that Hungary opened their border with Austria," he says.

A week or so after we arrived in Czechoslovakia, Hungary announced that it would allow members of the Communist Eastern Bloc through the frontier with Austria. Thousands of Czechoslovaks, East Germans, and Poles immediately raced for Hungary so that they could emigrate to the West. The other members of the Eastern Bloc tried to close down their borders with Hungary, but that proved difficult, since they had never thought to fortify frontiers within the Eastern Bloc.

I stand up and sling on my backpack. "Yeah. So?"

Freeman holds the door for me, like the gentleman nerd he is, and for a moment I think about Mike Reynolds, holding the elevator door for us at church, and I wonder if his little sister Chrissy is keeping her clothes on yet. But then Freeman starts talking and I have to pay attention. "So a bunch of East Germans were already in Czechoslovakia on their way to Hungary when the borders closed."

"Yeah," I say, as we make our way down the corridor past Cory's classroom. She gives a happy little wave when she sees us.

"Instead of going back home, where they would probably get in trouble for leaving in the first place, the East Germans remember that the West German government has a standing offer to give citizenship to any East German who wants it. So they decided to go to the West German Embassy in Prague and ask for political asylum. You know the embassy—right? It's that big yellow palace a couple of blocks north of the American Embassy that backs onto Petrin Hill."

"Okay," I say, wishing he would get to the point.

"So their friends heard about it—and now there's total gridlock in Malastrana because all these East German families are tootling down to Prague in their little Trabbies and Wartburgs and parking anywhere they can and making a run for the West German Embassy. Thousands of them showed up over the weekend. The embassy is going nuts. They don't have anywhere to put them."

"This the East Germans?" Sunil asks, coming into the room. "Dad and I went by last night to take them some tents. Hey, Merry, did you have a good time?"

"We did," she says, looking flushed and pretty, but I want to hear about the East Germans.

"They're camping out in the yard?" I say.

"Some of them," Sunil says. "They've made places for the children inside, but there are just too many people, and they keep coming. The StB is having a fit. As fast as they tow the abandoned cars away, more show up. And now so many newsmen have shown up from nonaligned countries that they don't dare arrest anyone."

Well. There's no way that I am going straight home from school now.

At the end of the day, I squish into the Nigerian Embassy's Benz with Abebi and all of her cousins. At the chancery, the aunts, dressed in bright cotton skirts and turbans, feed us fried plantains and herb tea in a sun porch draped with colorful batik hangings. I've never been here before and it is completely strange, with smells I don't recognize. But there's no time to make sense of it. Abebi tells her mother we have homework to do. We go into her bedroom and she finds the small plastic package we have come for. We take it into the bathroom. And then we are out of there, our backpacks bulging and bouncing against our backs.

The West German Embassy is only a few blocks away. We go the back way, on the secret path my father showed us that cuts through the woods to the garden where the people have come to take refuge. Some are playing soccer. Others toast links of bratwurst over bonfires, and still others strum guitars. Their clothes are tattered and dirty and their hair is uncombed, and I realize who they really are: the Gypsies. They have come to this garden so they can be safe from the police who want to make them sweep the streets and live in ugly crumbling housing projects.

Abebi and I hand them water balloons to throw at the StB through the back fence. Some people try to stop us, but I tell them we have diplomatic passports, and they stop.

When I get home and Mom and Dad start to yell, I go into my bedroom and pull the sheets over my head and read and read and read.

My favorite dreams are the ones when I can fly. Not way high up, not like a plane or anything. Skimming, really, just far enough above the ground so that I can go where I want to without rough bumps and jerky starts and stops. Skating is the closest thing I've found to flying. Ice skating is the best, of course, but blading is next best.

* * *

Abebi understands how important it is to keep moving. In Prague she goes to school and studies languages and plays soccer and hockey better than a lot of the boys. But soon her father's tour will be over and she will go home to Nigeria to the heat and the cooking and the flies and the aunts, and that will be it. So she throws back her head in this way she has, and her teeth are very white and her tongue is very pink, and we fly.

Wayne Gretzky says that the great ones never play where the puck is. They play according to where the puck will be. When you are moving, the edges are *supposed* to blur. When you are moving, it doesn't really matter where you are because you haven't gotten there yet. Moving feels safer to me than standing still.

Abebi is crying. The newsmen took pictures of us giving the Gypsies balloons, and her father is sending her back to her village. It is our last day together, and we go to Vyšehrad, the high castle where Prague was born. The Virgin Queen Libuše ruled here, in the city she named "Praha," which means threshold. As we look down to the Vltava and the spires below, Prague does seem a threshold, a misty gateway to I don't know what. Small lights flicker on the water and along the streets as the dusk gathers, but then they are swallowed in the mist. I turn away from the empty place they used to be.

We wander around the graves of poets and musicians, littered with flowers and votive candle offerings. The air smells of sulfur and smoke, the odor of winter in Prague. We are in a garden whose flowers are ashes and death. I tug Abebi away before she is ready, past the cathedral and into the flat rectangle of the bordering park. There are pathways here, and edges.

And statues, huge and calm and comforting. I don't pay attention to them at first, but Abebi loves them, especially the one of Libuše and the plowman Premysl who became her husband. They tower over us with their strong, simple faces and their silence. Abebi tells me that Libuše sleeps beneath our feet and will awaken when Bohemia is in its greatest danger. I look at my friend, at the smooth stretch of her black skin, her cheekbones, and her thick, kinky hair, and see her real face emerge, like Han Solo coming up through the carbonite. Abebi is Libuše, magnificent in her strength and her silence.

We do not speak of it, but I know she sees me recognize her.

We kneel before the queen and put on our flying shoes. The reason we have come to this high place is for the speed of our descent. The speed rushes through us and there are no empty spaces.

In the darkness, we are both magnificent.

I am alone again. I am looking for the Gypsies. Sometimes I can find them sweeping the streets, or smoking in a metro station. But although I listen for their music, I can't find it. Cory follows me around, so I can't hear the music. I tell her not to, but she does. I want the music, and she won't let me have it. Why won't she let me have it? Her face, her bad face, comes out more and more. I tell it to go away.

I am waiting now for hockey, so I can fly.

They show *Die Hard* to the marines on Saturday night. Dad takes me and Merry and Sunil and we talk and laugh and drink Cokes, but when the movie starts, the movement and noise assault me. I want to be in my bed. If I try hard enough, I am almost in my bed, but I cannot pull the covers far enough up to cover the movement and the noise.

I sit up straight. I am not in my bed. I am at the Dobry Den, the marines' bar in the basement of the embassy. We're watching a movie. But I'm having a hard time keeping up.

Karl, one of the henchmen, looks like an older version of the plainclothes policeman we talked to in Wenceslas Square. No, he is the policeman. Why is he in the movie? He dies. But then he isn't dead. Then he dies again. Where am I in this? I don't know. I ball my hands in the pockets of my jacket and push so that I will feel the edges of my body. But it isn't enough. I have a nail clipper in my pocket. I open it up and squeeze my finger between the levers.

It is such a little movement to move my other hand closer until my thumb is brushing the blades. I push it just a little harder against the clipper, and the blades slice it open with a little pop, a little crackle, like the hot dogs we ate on Wenceslas Square. It doesn't hurt, even though every time I stop pressing against it I can feel the wetness of more blood pooling from the cut. Now I know where one of my edges is.

After the movie, Dad takes us to Café Slavia and we eat stale pastries and he tells us stories about being a farm boy in Utah. We sit in a pool of light that pushes away the darkness, and my missing pieces float to our table. They turn in the air and settle gently into place, building me from the ground up.

Feet first, then knees and thighs, then stomach, then arms, neck, and head. I'm back.

It's the sacrament. The Czech saints stare at us with stony eyes as they pass the bread. We are bringing them danger. I take the bread and eat it. Jesus said that this was His body. When you take the sacrament, you are promising to share your life with Him, and He is promising to share His life with you. He is enough to make up for what you are not. I want that bread to fill up the emptiness, but how can it when we are bringing danger to His people?

Dad's arm is around Merry. Cory is on Mom's lap. But I am alone. My shoulders and hands quiver, ache almost. I bite my cheeks and close my eyes. An arm settles against my shoulders. I don't open my eyes, because I know that if I look, I will not see Him, but He is there.

The Gypsies are gone. Ten thousand souls, gone. Like the Jews of Mikulov. Like Lexy and Toby and Abebi. They have left me. Everyone is smiling because the East Germans have escaped to the West. But when I walk by the square where they used to camp, all I can see is emptiness.

I am falling. There is nowhere I can go, nothing I can do, no position I can assume to stop the falling. I go to my nest and read my old friends—Susan Cooper and Jean Little and Elizabeth George Speare, books stained with juice from Grandpop's grapes and crumbs from Nana's cakes. I can't fall when I am someone else.

I see Libuše crossing the threshold without me. She has Anežka's face, and she doesn't wait.

I wish Toby were here, but she's home chasing squirrels in the vineyard. I want to feel her hot, wet breath in my face. I want to put my feet under her silky coat. But Mom and Dad wouldn't let us bring her. And even though they say they are worried about me, they won't take us back to the way things were.

I grab Dad's car key and Merry's Tracy Chapman tape. Someone needs to find the Gypsies and teach them how to fly. I blast the song about a car fast enough to fly away as the hills speed by.

I am flying. It's hard to feel like you are flying in Czechoslovakia. That's why skating matters so much. But today there is sun, and the road curves before me like a runway into space. I tell Anežka that I am going to take the Gypsies and we will fly away. She is smiling at me.

When I get to Brno I have to drive slowly because I don't know the signs, and then I see the market near the railroad station. There are skates there, skates for the Gypsies, and I buy them all with my coat and my gloves and my boots, which I really don't need because I have heavy woolen socks, and then I take them to the Gypsies.

Here are the fruit trees, their trunks painted white so we will not lose the way. I love Anežka for making sure that the trunks are painted white, so I know where the edges are. I turn to her to thank her for this gracious act, but she isn't there.

It stops. It all stops.

The tape doesn't work anymore, and my head hurts. I get out of the car and find the pond, and I lay out the skates carefully so they can choose the right sizes. Then I wait, but they don't come. I wait and wait. It's cold, but I have to wait for the Gypsies. They need people who will wait for them, who will see them and not leave.

It is nighttime, and I can see the moon on the ice. The strangeness is so thick in my chest that I can barely breathe. There are more moons moving through the trees. Doors slam.

It's the Gypsies!

No, it's Anežka. And I can feel her strong arms and smell her warm breath.

"Anežka!" I say. "I knew you'd come!"

Someone is with her. Josef.

"I don't want him here," I say, beginning to cry. "He will scare away the Gypsies."

"He is going," she says. "Do not worry. He's going to get help."

"But he has to help the Gypsies," I say.

"He will," she croons, and she sounds like Mom talking to Cory when she was a baby. "He knows all about taking care of the Gypsies. But now, let us take care of you. It looks like you have bumped your head."

She takes off her scarf and pats at my head, and I jerk away. "That was a long time ago," I say. "And it's better. They promised me it would get better."

"Of course it is," she says, shrugging out of her coat and wrapping it around me. She takes off her coat and boots and puts them on me. "Of course you are better."

"Look what I brought!" I say, showing her all the skates. "This is how they can fly."

"So who can fly, Jude?" she asks, looking into my face so that I know that she is really listening.

"The Gypsies," I say. "The Gypsies." Now that Anežka is here, some of the strangeness is blowing away, and I can breathe again. "I was quiet so I could hear their music, but I've been waiting and waiting and they still haven't come. Did I do it wrong?"

"No, sweetheart," she says. "You did exactly right." And we sit and rock together and wait for the Gypsies.

NUREMBERG, GERMANY

November 1989

QUESTIONS

A dark face wakes me. I think it is Abebi, but this voice has Jamaican music in it.

I answer her questions sleepily. Yes, my name is Jude Wheelock. I am fifteen years old. I have no medical allergies.

My head hurts. My questioner is wearing a uniform.

"Where am I?"

"You are in the U.S. military hospital in Nuremberg," she says. "In Germany."

I turn away, too tired to ask why.

When I wake up again, Mom and Dad are there. She is crying. He is holding her. Neither one of them sees me, so I close my eyes and go away again.

The sound of a woman opening the blinds wakes me up. She is backlit by the bright, sunny day, and she shimmers around her edges. When she steps away from the window, I see she is my mother.

"Good morning, sleepyhead," she says, giving me a hug. "That was certainly a dramatic way of getting out of school. How do you feel?"

I shrug. When she bends down to get something, I turn my head so that I can smell where her perfume lingers on my shoulder.

"Dad and I brought you some clothes," she says, and hefts a duffel bag onto a Formica table pushed against the wall.

"Dad?" I say. My brain is thick, like it's filled with chocolate pudding. "Is he here too?"

"Yep. He's down in the lobby trying to put a call in to Mrs. Marek at school." She fusses with the bag and lifts out my jeans, a T-shirt, my favorite sweatshirt. "Are you up to getting dressed?"

"Yeah," I say, and swing my legs over the edge of the bed.

Then somehow Mom is there instead of over by the bag. "A little wobbly?" she says. "Don't push it, honey. You banged your head pretty hard and they've given you medication to … to … calm you down."

"Maybe I'll wait a minute," I say. "Is Dad in a hurry to go?"

"No, I don't think so," she says. Her voice sounds strange through the pudding in my head.

Someone opens the door. It's Dad, holding a dumb little bunch of droopy flowers that he must have gotten at a gift shop. "Hey, honey. It's awfully good to see the whites of your eyes." He comes over to kiss me and I see that he hasn't shaved. I don't think I've ever seen my father unshaven before.

"You're all bristly," I say.

"We were in a hurry to get here," Dad says. "Forgot my razor." He drags a couple of chairs over and puts one on each side of the bed, for Mom and himself. "Sweetheart, there's something we need to tell you."

I look at his face, and at Mom's. Something bad is happening. I know something bad is happening, but I can't feel anything through the chocolate pudding in my brain.

Mom takes my hand. But it's not really my hand. I start to tell her but then don't, because I don't want her to be embarrassed by her mistake.

"Jude," Dad says. He clears his throat. "Jude, honey, the doctors want you to stay here for a while."

"Why?" I say. "I'm fine."

"They'd like to talk to you some more about the accident."

I look back and forth between them, suddenly frightened. "Are they going to arrest me?"

"No, sweetheart," Dad says. "Nothing like that. But you were pretty upset when Josef and his sister found you. The doctors just want to make sure that—" He hesitates.

The room tips as my pudding-thick brain finally realizes what it is that he cannot bring himself to say.

"That I'm not crazy," I hear myself say. I can't get my breath. They're going to leave me here. They saw. They knew I was falling, but they didn't tell me. I start to cry.

I didn't know, I want to tell them. *I didn't understand.* But I can't push the words through the strange clear jelly that shimmers between me and them. It's back again. It never really went away.

Of course Mom and Dad are going. They have to keep themselves safe from me. They have to. They have other children who need them.

"Jude," Mom says. "Jude. Look at me."

I do. Her eyes are wet.

"Honey, we know that this has been a hard move for you. Prague is a hard place for everyone right now. If there is something these people can do to help you so that you don't hurt so much, we want them to do it."

"Don't leave me here," I say. "Please. I'll be good. I promise."

"We know, honey," Mom says. "We know you'll be good."

Someone comes into the room behind me. I wait for Dad to tell the person to go away, that our family is talking and we're not finished. But he doesn't.

"Jude," Dad says. I won't look at him or the person who came into the room, but Dad keeps talking anyway. "This is Dr. Tanner. He's going to spend some time getting to know you. Honey, listen. This is important. We want you to tell him the truth. We know that you have been mad at us some of the time. It's okay if you tell him that. It's okay to tell him exactly what you feel."

"Hi, Jude," Dr. Tanner says. He walks over to Mom's side of the bed and puts out his hand so that Mom lets go. He's wearing one of those big school rings, like all the marines do.

I am angry that she is letting me go. I don't look at him.

He squats down so that his face is right in front of mine. "I'm Dr. Tanner. And we're going to see what we can do to make you feel better."

He's a pipsqueak, one of those little white-bread, Middle America, uniformed pipsqueaks. His mouth is too wide and his nose is too big and his hair is straight and would flop in his eyes if he didn't have one of those marine-type haircuts.

My eyes slide away as he tries to shake my hand. I make it as much like a cold, limp fish as I can. The first thing Mom and Dad told us when we moved to New York was, "When people shake your hand, don't be afraid to use a nice, firm grip, and look them straight in the eye."

"Jude," says Dad. "We've got to go now."

His words are sharp as knives, but his face is a blur. "Dad, don't go," I say, so frightened I am afraid that my bones will fly apart. "Dad, you can't go. Please don't leave me here!"

I am crying again, like the night with the brownies, and I can't stop. I've got to stop, so that they will see it's safe to take me with them. "Please!" I beg. "I'll keep my room clean! I'll come straight home from school! I'll do anything! But you can't leave me here!"

"I'm so sorry, honey," Mom whispers, but she's standing up.

I try to get to her, to touch her so she'll remember that I'm here, that I'm real, but Dr. Tanner grabs me.

"I'm not crazy! I'm not crazy! You can't do this! You can't leave me here!" I shriek.

Dad is crying. I've never seen him cry before, and part of me is happy that I have done this. "Honey, I'd like to give you a blessing, but I can't unless you calm down. Honey, please. I don't want to leave you here without a blessing."

I am fighting Dr. Tanner, kicking and scratching and trying

to bite him, but the little pipsqueak is stronger than he looks and the pudding has spread to my legs and arms. They've drugged me, I realize, and I'm inside a horrible nightmare that will not end. "Let me go! Let me go! Don't leave me here!"

"It's probably best if you just leave," Dr. Tanner says to my parents.

And they do.

"Dr. Tanner is ready to see you."

I stare at the nurse standing beside my bed. I cannot speak.

"Can you hear me?" she says. Then she looks at me again and her voice changes. "Dr. Tanner is a good doctor," she says. "He will help you feel better. Why don't you come with me now?"

And I want to. I want to leave this place. But I cannot.

Her brown fingers, brown like Abebi, brown like Lola who made our apartment clean and safe, are on my shoulder. "Come with me now," she says again.

I want to. I want her fingers to make it possible. But I can't.

Then Dr. Tanner is there. "We're going to see if we can find some medication that will help you feel better," he says, peering down at me from under his hairy blond eyebrows.

"How long?" I manage.

"Before you are feeling better? I don't know," he says. "Anywhere from a few days to a few weeks."

Too long. That's much too long.

The nurse helps me sit up with her brown hands. She puts pills in my mouth and then holds a cup of water to my lips. Some water splashes on my stomach, and with a jerk the creature inside me wakes up.

ALONE

There is no lock on my door. People in uniforms come in and out whenever they want to. They take my blood and my urine. They measure and record and assess. But no matter how they chart the data, the experiment is failing.

I can feel the darkness coming for hours before it is actually here. The dread grows and grows, crushing me, squeezing the lifeblood from me as though I am one of Grandpop's grapes. The agony will not end. It has always been, and always will be. I tell myself that the sun will rise again, that things will be better in the morning, but I know it is a lie. I try to pray, but the words circle in my brain until they are gone, too.

When I finally drift off into a drugged sleep, I float alone through the dark, endless space. Waves crash over my head, beating against me, scouring my filthy body against the rough sand until no part of me remains. Our New York elevator swallows me, taking me up, up, up beyond our floor while I jab fruitlessly at the buttons, only to break and dash me against the subway tracks that lurk beneath the building, tracks guarded by frontier police with clumsy guns that shoot fire through me.

Dr. Tanner says that dreams like these are normal when your body is going on or off medications. It doesn't feel normal to me. Nothing is normal. Not the fake scrambled eggs. Not the institutional-smelling bathrooms that have showers but no tubs. Not the hospital sheets or the plastic utensils or the nurses who are always spying on me. Nothing happening to me is normal.

"It will get better," Dr. Tanner says. "I promise. I just don't know when. And we can't let you go until we are sure you are safe."

"I have been abandoned by my family hundreds of miles from home in a hospital built by the Nazis," I say. "What is safe about that?"

"It seems safer to me than driving across a Communist country without a license and crashing into a tree."

That's a low blow.

"Look, Jude, it sounds like a lot of painful things have happened recently. You want to tell me about any of them?"

I pick at the torn, infected place on my thumb. *Not really.* "What do you want from me?" I ask.

"Absolutely nothing," he says. "I neither want nor need anything from you, except to help. So there's nothing to worry about, nothing you have to keep back because it might hurt or scare me. It won't."

I'm offended by his implication. "Our family isn't like that."

"Like what?"

"Our family doesn't keep secrets. We tell people when we love them. And we yell at them when they make us angry."

He nods. "You and your parents seem to have a really healthy relationship."

"Damn straight," I say.

"So how does it make you feel that they've left you here?"

His words have sucked all the air out of my lungs. "What?"

"You said you'd been abandoned by your family. How does that make you feel?"

I look at his eyes, which are kind of soft, like he really wants to know. They're brown and squinty under hairy, bleached-out eyebrows, nothing like my family's round blue ones. And we all have dark, neat eyebrows. That makes it easier. Less like I'm telling on them.

"They had to," I say. "They didn't want to."

"Okay," he says. "But what you're telling me is why they did what they did, and that's not what I asked. What I want to know is how you feel about them leaving you here."

"Fine," I say.

"That is a lie," he says calmly.

I can't believe he has said that to me. "Excuse me?"

"I saw a young girl kicking and screaming and completely out of control. That didn't look like 'fine' to me."

"You're being very rude," I say.

"I'm just trying to understand your feelings."

"It's none of your business."

"Why does the idea of someone wanting to understand you bother you so much?" he says.

"Because you won't."

"How do you know? I'm a pretty smart guy."

"Well, for one thing I'm a Mormon."

"So?"

"Well, I know what *my* reaction would be if I had a mental patient who told me that she believed that God and Jesus Christ appeared to Joseph Smith and gave him golden plates."

"What would it be?"

"Look, the point is, if you're not religious, you're not going to get it."

"Who says I'm not religious?" he asks.

That shuts me up for a second. "Are you?"

He shrugs. "That's not something I'm going to tell you. But this is your time. If you don't want to talk about being Mormon, we won't."

"I don't," I say flatly.

"All right," he says, in a pleasant, calm voice.

"And if you don't get being Mormon, then you can't possibly understand me at all."

He raises one of his hairy blond eyebrows. "At all? I won't be able to understand you *at all*? There is not one thing about you that I could possibly understand?"

"Not fully," I say.

"Fair enough," he says. "How about ninety percent? Still too much? How about eighty?"

"Maybe," I say, grudgingly.

"Your parents tell me that you're good at science," he says, leaning forward.

"Yeah, I guess," I say.

"I want you to try a thought experiment with me."

I make a noncommittal noise.

"Say that you had lived three times as long as you have. Do you think you'd have learned anything more than you know right now?"

"Maybe."

He looks at me.

"Okay. Yes," I say ungraciously, knowing where he is going with this and not liking it.

"Say you spent twelve of those extra years doing pretty much nothing but studying the ways people make sense of the world. Say you've heard or seen or read thousands and thousands of life stories. Is there something in there you might have learned?"

"Maybe."

"Look, Jude, I'll be honest with you. It's true that there are some things about you I may never understand. It is also true that, given the same information, you and I might make different choices. But please believe me when I tell you that the only reason I am here is to help you become the person you want to be, not the person I want you to be. There are things I can suggest that might be useful to you. Whether you decide to take my advice is totally your business. But it might be useful to have a friend who's had a little more life experience than you have."

Then, just as I am beginning to feel interested, he glances at the clock on his desk that I can't see. "That's all the time we have for today. One of the nurses will bring you supper, then—"

I sit bolt upright. "That's it? You go into this big song and dance and then time's *up*?"

He looks at me, his eyebrows raised. "You have fifty minutes, and that fifty minutes is up. Now, on Thursdays I go to Vienna, but I'll be back on Friday and I'll see you then."

"I thought you said it would be once a week."

"It will be," he says. "But we can see each other more often while you're here."

Things still aren't normal. I tell this to Mrs. Montgomery and Anežka. I am not supposed to have visitors until my medications have stabilized, but they find a way in. Neither one of them would leave me here the way my parents did. Mrs. Montgomery shows me where she goes when the doctors come so that they can't see her. She is there with her candles, and when we are sure no one will see we are going to light some. She tells me that Merry is here looking for me, but I cannot find her. I think it is that nurse who is hiding her from me.

The meds aren't working. So they try others. Mrs. Montgomery doesn't know how to get past the others. Now I am really alone.

"Why won't you let her come?" I sob to Dr. Tanner. "We were going to light the candles."

"Who?" he says. "Your mother? You know we've asked her not to come until we've got your meds stabilized."

Remembering that no one is supposed to come makes me so angry that I stop crying. "Not my mother," I say as nastily as I can. "You think you're so smart, but you don't have any idea what I'm talking about."

He doesn't say anything.

Just to show him how stupid he is being, I tell him, "My mother wouldn't come anyhow. She's way too busy."

"Too busy doing what?"

I shrug. "Studying. Taking care of the other kids. You know."

"No, I don't know. What would be more important to her than to be here with you?"

I look at him. Sometimes he is not very smart. "Lots of things. Her research. Taking care of the house. You know. You have to wait your turn."

"Do you think her research and housework are more important to her than you are?"

I squirm in my seat. "When it's my turn, it's really good."

"So sometimes your mom can make you really happy."

I think about the birthday parties, the picnics at my grandparents', the Band-Aids and kisses when I got hurt. "Yeah. She understands me. She makes me feel safe."

"Can you think of a specific time when she did that?"

I pick at the torn place on my thumb. "When I woke up here."

"So you didn't feel scared when you woke up in the hospital because your mother was here."

"Yeah."

"And when she left you here, the scary feelings came back."

"Yeah. I guess," I say. There are no windows in this office, which really bothers me.

"So when you feel bad, your mom could probably help you feel better."

"If she wanted to. But sometimes it's not my turn."

"So what does she do when it stops being your turn?"

"She does the next thing."

"What does she do about you?"

"Nothing."

"Nothing?"

I shrug. "She forgets me, I guess. Because it's time for the next thing."

"Jude, do you really believe that your mother stops thinking about you when you are not there? That she stops loving you?"

"Your office really needs a window."

"Jude?"

I stand up. "I think it's time to go now."

"Sit down," Dr. Tanner says. "We've got plenty of time. Do you think your mother stops loving you when she's not there? Why would you think that?"

"Because," I say. "If she remembered me, she would make it better. But it's not getting better. It's just getting worse. Everyone keeps leaving." I can't sit still. I am rocking back and forth.

"Jude. It's okay," I hear Dr. Tanner saying. "You're in my office. You're safe. These are just feelings. Feelings can't hurt you."

I laugh and cry. "Oh, yeah? Well, someone forgot to tell them that," I say.

Dr. Tanner doesn't say anything.

I cry for a while, but then I get tired, so I stop.

"We haven't talked about Merry yet," Dr. Tanner says once I stop gulping. "Being a twin is an intimate thing."

I close my eyes. I don't want to talk anymore. I want to go to bed. "Isn't the time up yet?"

"Not yet," Dr. Tanner says. "What's it like to be a twin?"

"We're fraternal twins," I say, my eyes still closed. "So we're not really the same."

"No two people are ever exactly the same," he says.

He doesn't get it. "She's older," I say.

"Yeah? So?"

"She was ready."

Dr. Tanner looks confused. "Ready for what?"

I remember what Dad said. That it was okay to tell the truth. "When we were born, she was ready. But I wasn't. It wasn't anyone's *fault*," I say. "No one *planned* it that way. It just happened."

"What happened?"

"I couldn't breathe. My lungs weren't ready." I am talk-talk-talking again. Maybe it is the drugs. "I think maybe that's how it started."

"How what started?"

"It's like my edges never set," I say dreamily. I'm in that tired, floaty place that you go after you've had a good cry. "Have you ever noticed how some people seem to have a line between them and everything else, like a skin or something, that keeps them safe?"

"I've never heard it described quite that way," he says. "But I know what you mean."

"I don't have that skin," I say. I close my eyes again. "I wish I did."

He has taken my skin away.

"Why do you make it so difficult?" I ask him.

"Believe me, Jude, I'm working as hard as I can to make it easier."

I look at him and know that he believes that what he is saying is true. "Other people don't hurt like this, do they?" I wait for his answer, my heart beating in my throat.

"No," he says. "They don't."

"What am I supposed to do?" I explode. *"I'm sad, I'm sad, oh Mommy, I'm sad, take care of me, Mommy. How much of that do you think she could stand?"*

"So you feel that knowing the truth about your pain would overwhelm people?"

I put my hands over my ears and curl up so that his words won't hurt me. I rock myself so that they can't hurt me.

"Jude," he says. "Jude. Come back."

I shake my head and rock faster.

"Open your eyes and look at me, Jude. Do I look over-whelmed?"

I open my eyes and look at him. He looks back, an ordinary, boring-looking guy. He's just ordinary. Vanilla. Normal. Nothing special.

It has never occurred to me that "nothing special" is another way of saying "something you can count on." "Nothing special" is like the black stone lab tables in Dr. Palmer's classroom. You don't have to be careful of "nothing special." You can spill on nothing special, and put hot things on it, and it won't matter. It's there to be used.

"You can tell me anything you want," he says. "You are safe here. "

"I think something might be wrong with me," I whisper to the torn place on my thumb.

"I think it might be time to have your parents come in for a meeting," Dr. Tanner says. "Would that be all right with you?"

BORDERLINE

"Jude suffers from an illness called Borderline Personality Disorder," Dr. Tanner tells us.

We're sitting in a different office for the Big Conference today, Mom and Dad and me, one that's much nicer than the usual one. My parents sit stiffly on the edge of their chairs. They look awkward and out of place in the middle of the fake mahogany veneer. It's all wrong that my family and Dr. Tanner are in the same place. Although I wanted them to come, now I wish they would leave. I want to go back to our regular room that is banged up and ordinary and only big enough for two.

The whole thing is so weird that I'm not paying much attention to what Dr. Tanner is saying. But Mom squeezes my hand hard. I look at her face and see that she is about to cry. I look at Dad. He looks absolutely furious, which almost never happens. I shrink back in my seat, knowing that everyone must wish I would stop causing trouble and just go away.

"How wedded are you to this particular diagnosis, Doctor?" Dad asks, practically biting off the words.

But Dr. Tanner isn't rattled. "I'm not wedded to it. But it seems to fit." He turns to me. "It sounds like your parents are familiar with BPD, but you'd probably like to know a little bit about it. When bad things happen to most of us, we can remember happier times and use those memories to help soothe ourselves. But when people with BPD are frightened or stressed, they literally cannot remember what it is like to be happy.

"Many—but not all—of the people who suffer from BPD were beaten or abused as children," Dr. Tanner goes on. "But Jude seems to be the exception here." He gives Dad the same calm smile he's used on me a hundred times, and I feel the tension in the room ease. "Jude's premature birth was a substantial trauma. It may have been the precipitating factor. Or there may be other genetic or environmental vulnerabilities that we simply don't understand yet."

"So what does this mean for my daughter?" Dad asks.

"I'm not going to lie to you," Dr. Tanner says. "This is a tough one, both for the patients and for the people who love them. Because they seem to function pretty well most of the time, when patients become symptomatic it's tempting to think that it's something they are doing on purpose. That Jude, for example, could control her impulsivity or her sadness if she really wanted to. That is not accurate. This is an illness, just like diabetes or hemophilia. There are structural abnormalities in Jude's brain and in her brain chemistry that inhibit her ability to hear praise and intensify her feelings of fear and distrust. They also make it very difficult for her to control impulsive behaviors."

So my brain is defective. I say the words over and over again, like a lullaby, but they mean nothing to me. My brain is defective. My brain is defective. They're just sounds. *Mmmmm yyyyyyyy bbbbbbb rrrrrrr aaaaaa—*. They're just sounds, like the noises babies sing to themselves in their cribs. They don't mean anything.

Dr. Tanner is still talking. "The good news is that Jude is smart, she has a supportive family, and we've got a diagnosis before risky secondary behaviors have gotten out of hand. It's the secondary behaviors, the things patients do to distract themselves from their pain—gambling, drugs, things like that—that really get them into trouble. Jude appears to have done some minor cutting, but that's all. Which is very good news. She is showing the symptoms a little younger than most—the move may have accelerated things—but her youth and the strong behavioral code of your religion have helped protect her from a lot of potentially serious complications."

"So aside from the cutting, she hasn't engaged in any secondary behaviors," Mom says, like she's trying to memorize the words. "And that's a good thing."

She looks scared. I've never seen my mother look scared before.

"It's *very* good," Dr. Tanner says.

"So what we need to do is keep her away from those secondary behaviors," Mom says.

"That's certainly a fine place to start," Dr. Tanner says. "It's also really important for her to stay on her meds, and to see a therapist you have confidence in at least once a week.

More would be better, especially at first, but your living situation complicates that."

"Would it be better if we took her back to the U.S.?" Mom asks.

"I don't think so," he says. "If you were going back to your life in New York, that would be one thing. But Utah is going to require all kinds of adjustments. No, I think it's probably better to continue as you have begun."

He keeps talking, but I'm not listening anymore. New York is gone. Thatcher and Lexy and little Chrissy Reynolds are gone. Forever. Even if they wanted to, Mom and Dad really can't take me back. The polished wood table in front of me blurs.

I am alone, and I am frightened. Dimly, I feel someone moving. An arm comes down around my shoulders, and I remember the sacrament service in Prague. Then I get a whiff of aftershave, and I snuggle in against my dad.

"Is this a permanent condition?"

I feel his words move from his chest through his arm to me. And I can feel all three of us holding our breath as we wait for the answer.

"It is extremely likely that Jude will struggle with many of these issues all her life," Dr. Tanner says. "But I also think that it is reasonable to expect that, given time and therapy, Jude will not only feel much better than she has, but that she has a good shot at leading a life that is essentially normal. There will certainly be setbacks and rough patches. But they should get less severe and less frequent with time."

"Or so we hope," Mom says.

"So we reasonably expect," Dr. Tanner says. "At the same time, of course, it's important to be realistic about the process. It won't be easy—either for Jude or for you. Jude is in an enormous amount of pain, and people who are in that kind of pain can be difficult to live with. The thing you and she will both have to remember when things get tough is that there are biological reasons for what is going on."

Biological reasons. I'm defective. My brain is defective. How am I supposed to fix myself if it's my mind that's broken?

The words are too deep inside me to utter. I look at my parents, willing them to speak my question for me, and then I see what I have done.

Dad's mouth is working like an old man's. Mom's eyes are dazed and frightened. I have broken their hearts. I didn't mean to, but I did.

THE **WALL**

I am not allowed to go home until they are sure the antipsychotic medication is working and random people aren't appearing out of my brain to keep me company. I pretend to be disappointed, but I am not.

Mom and Dad brought a big suitcase with my rollerblades, a coat, my Walkman and some tapes, and a bunch of homework. My mind doesn't have room for the homework, but the tapes and the blades help the time go faster.

The nights are the worst. Even though the dreams are slowly getting better, I'm having a hard time sleeping. I wake up about two o'clock in the morning and lie in bed and think about the unlocked door and all the stupid things I've done to get me in this room stripped of all sharp objects and reeking of disinfectant. Maybe if I hadn't said anything about having to wait my turn with Mom they would have let me leave. Or that stuff about Merry. I lie there while the moonlight whispers that other people get BPD because people were mean to them. They thought that that was the way the world was. So they can unthink it.

My BPD happened because that's the way I was made. By God. He made me this way on purpose. Why would He want me to have a body that hurts me? I'm afraid of the answer to that question, so I close my mind while I feel myself falling, falling, falling, until it's morning at last.

They let Mom visit on Wednesday. She brings me two six-packs of Coke and bags of apples and oranges and brownies and chocolate chip cookies and flying saucers that they made for me during Family Night, and a big bowl of tuna fish just the way I like it that the nurses say I can keep in their fridge. Cory has sent her camera so that I can take pictures to show them where I am living. We go for a long walk through the grounds and get permission to buy hot chocolate in the village.

When we drive out of the gates there are too many people and too many lights. The hot chocolate is delicious, but after a few sips I am ready to go home to my quiet bed. I do not cry when Mom says goodbye—although she does.

I lie on my bed, almost too tired to breathe. It is hard to be with people when you aren't who you thought you were.

"Merry was never very good at hide-and-seek," I tell Dr. Tanner.

"Why's that?" he asks.

"She didn't know how to listen. If you listen, you can hear where people are going. I don't think she would ever have figured that out if I hadn't told her."

He nods.

"She didn't learn how to ride a bike or pump on the swings or roller skate at the right age," I say. I know I shouldn't tell him these things, but I can't stop. "She still can't go hand-over-hand on the monkey bars. Or whistle. We'll be sitting on the bus or something and I'll see her puckering up her lips. I know she's trying, but nothing ever comes out."

"Can you whistle?" Dr. Tanner asks.

"Yep," I say. I whistle some Bach. He looks impressed.

"I used to get mad at her," I say. "I pretended not to, but I did. I thought she must be doing it on purpose. It really bugged me."

"I imagine that it bugged her, too," he says.

"She always said it did, but I didn't believe her. I pretended to, but I didn't."

"So Merry still can't whistle."

"No."

"But she learned how to ride a bike eventually."

"Yeah."

"And how to pump on the swings. And she learned how to listen to where people were going when you played hide-and-seek."

"Yeah."

"She's still not an athlete."

"No."

"Probably never will be," he says. "At least not like you."

"No," I say, feeling disloyal. "Not like me."

"Sounds like she gets along okay, though," he says, putting on his reading glasses and looking down at his yellow pad.

"What did you say?"

He looks at me over his glasses, reminding me, absurdly, of Josef calculating the bill in the wine cellar. "Sounds like she manages just fine anyway."

Dannie, the Jamaican nurse, tells me that Merry and Dad have come to see me, but I'm not ready.

"Seems to me lots of people in this hospital would give their right arm for some good folks like that to come visiting," she says.

I turn my back to her, wishing she would go away.

"They're not going to hurt you," she says. "But if you lie there and don't come down, you'll be hurting them."

After a while, I get up and go down to meet them. There is a big, full-length mirror between the elevators in the lobby, and I see their reflections before I see them. Merry looks so smooth and pretty and grown-up that I want to stop and just look at her for a while. But I can't, because she is turning away to talk to a patient.

Then I realize that that patient is me. I look ... sick. My hair is dirty and uncombed, there are yellow bruised places under my eyes, and my shoelaces are untied.

"Hey, twin," Merry says. She gives me a big hug like I am not scary at all and whispers in my ear, "I've missed you." But I see in her eyes that I have broken her heart, too.

We walk slowly around the grounds while Merry gets me caught up on school gossip. Sophy and Ahmed are going out. "Oh! I nearly forgot. Cory sent you something."

Merry rummages in her purse, frowning. "She wanted to send her cowboy boots, but Mom wouldn't let her. Then she found out that Mr. Montgomery had been in Berlin on Thursday and had brought Kate a piece of the Wall, so she talked Kate into breaking off a little piece to send you. Here." She holds out a baggie with a chunk of concrete in it.

I stare at the concrete, and then at Merry, trying to make sense of her story.

She shakes the bag impatiently. "The Wall," she says. "This is a piece of the Wall."

"What wall?"

"You haven't heard about the Wall?"

I shake my head, feeling stupid. But then I see it doesn't matter. They are smiling, no, *beaming*, delighted that they are the ones who get to tell me.

"They've taken down the Berlin Wall," Dad says. "Night before last. Honecker, the East German prime minister, had to resign after he let all those émigrés slip through his fingers. Thursday night, the new government held a press conference to announce that they were ending all travel restrictions. A reporter asked when, and the guy kind of blurted out, 'Er, now, I guess.' And that was it. The Wall came down that night."

"There's no more Berlin Wall?" I say, looking back and forth between them.

"Not much of one," Dad says. "People brought their sledgehammers and relegated it, as Karl Marx himself would say, to the dustbin of history."

I look at the chunk of concrete I am holding in my hand. "This was part of the Wall?"

"Yep," Merry says.

I can't get over that something so big and evil is gone, just like that. The reason that all those people came to Prague and camped in the cold, the reason Abebi got sent home, the reason people have been shot and killed and families have been divided, is gone, just like that. Not gotten around. Overcome.

I run my fingers over the hard edges, then hand it back, reluctantly. "They won't let me keep it."

"Why not?" Merry asks.

"Because I could use it to hurt myself," I say.

"Oh."

"Tell Cory to take care of it for me until I get home. And tell her I love it. Tell her it's the best present anyone's ever given me."

I want to go home. But home is in Prague, and bad things happen in Prague. My mind does bad things in Prague.

Where else can I go?

There is nowhere else.

By the time I see Dr. Tanner on Monday I feel like I am going to explode, like my brain is going to burn a hole right through my skull. The tension has been building and building and there is no way to get rid of it.

"I hate this!" I shriek at him. "I don't want this! It's not fair! It's too hard! Make it stop!" I want to turn off my brain. I want it to stop and let me rest. But there's no button. No cord to unplug. All I can do is kill it dead. I bang my head against the wall as hard and fast as I can.

"I can't make it stop," Dr. Tanner says. "But I can remind

you that you're talking about feelings. And feelings can't do anything. You're the one with the body, not them."

"I want to make them to go away."

"Sorry to be the one to tell you this," he says, not looking sorry at all, "but that's not up to you."

"What?"

"You can't stop your feelings," he says. "No one can. The best you can do is to get a good look at them, find out if they have anything to teach you, and then move on."

"Easy for you to say."

He leans forward. "Pay attention, Judith Grace, because I'm about to say something really wise. If you want to get better, you're going to have to accept the world on its own terms and save your energy for what you can fix. Someone who has gone blind can yell and scream all they want, but it won't do a thing for their vision. It's not until they start working with what they've got, until they start to study Braille and get a guide dog, that things are going to improve for them."

"So you're saying I'm blind."

"What I'm saying is, yes, you are in terrible pain a lot of the time. It's not your fault. It's nothing you did. But it's not anyone else's fault, either. Asking why isn't going to change anything. Getting stuck in blaming yourself or the people around you won't help. Neither will pretending you're not suffering when you are, or acting out to distract yourself. Because the feelings are still in charge."

"Like the Wall," I say, slowly.

"What?"

"The Wall. The Berlin Wall."

He shakes his head, not understanding.

"It seemed so big and powerful," I say. "And it was. People died because of it. Or became cowards. Or liars. But nothing worked. Until people were brave enough to overcome it."

"Last Thursday, you mean."

I shake my head impatiently. "No, not last Thursday. That was the easy part. *They* had permission."

"Ahh," he says.

"It was the families," I say. "The families who were brave enough to say no, they wouldn't. Can you imagine what that must have been like? Putting it all on the line like that when no one had ever done it before—well, maybe a handful, like in that Disney movie, but basically, they knew they had no chance. They *knew* they had no chance. They *knew* it. Because they were the ones who had survived, who had been around to see what happened when the Wall won. But they went anyway. It was cold and winter was coming, but they didn't care—they packed everything they could into cars made of old carpets and glue, and when one border closed they found another, and then when that ran out they abandoned their cars—the only things that had a reasonable chance of taking them anywhere—in the middle of a foreign city and ran as hard as they could, without any guarantee that anyone was waiting to catch them."

By now I'm talking so loud and fast that I have to stop and pant for a minute.

"How did they do it?" I plead with him. "Tell me. Please. How?"

"Figure that one out," he says, "and the battle's won." He closes his yellow pad and caps his pen. "That's all we have time for today."

I hate those words.

THE SLAV **EPIC**

Mom picks me up before lunch on Tuesday, which is okay because Dr. Tanner and I have a phone session scheduled for Wednesday at 4:00. That's only twenty-eight hours away. I can last for twenty-eight hours.

I'm glad to see it's the good old Volvo parked at the entrance, not the school's shiny Benz. Mom sees me looking at it. "Now we look more like the natives," she says. I see that the front left panel is now black instead of dusty blue.

My stomach lurches. "Was that because of me?" I ask.

"Yep."

"Was it expensive?"

"Not your problem," Mom says, throwing my suitcase in the back, where it joins Cory's rollerblades. "*Your* problem is to decide what we are going to do for lunch. How does a Big Mac sound?"

"Great!" I say, making an effort. I slam the rear door closed and climb into the dusty, cluttered front seat. The Volvo does not smell like it has been disinfected *ever*, which is A-OK with me.

German Big Macs do not taste like American Big Macs. Plus you have to pay extra for ketchup packets. There are too many lights and people and noises. I throw my food away after a couple of bites so we can get back to the car, and then I sleep most of the way to Prague.

I wake up as the city closes in around us. I stretch and look around blearily. "This isn't the way to our house," I say, confused.

"I know, honey. We're picking up Cory at school."

School. The word itself weighs me down so that I can hardly breathe. "I don't have to go in or see anyone or anything?" I manage to say.

Mom gives me a quick glance. "No, honey, not this week."

I sink back against the car seat, relieved.

Cory is happy to see me, and I am happy to see her. But it is hard for me to talk. After a few minutes, I close my eyes, and when we get home I go straight to bed and pull the covers over my head.

Now that I am back in my own bed, I can read again. The words stay on the page instead of breaking up and jumping around. No one bothers me except to say good night or good morning or do I want to come for breakfast. I don't, so they bring it to me.

When I talk to Dr. Tanner, he says that it's normal that things are loud and confusing, and that it will get better. And he'll see me Saturday morning. Sixty-six hours. It's sixty-six hours. I can last for sixty-six more hours.

Wednesday night after Cory is in bed, Mom comes into

our room to give me my meds. I swallow them obediently, impatient to get back to *The Count of Monte Cristo*. But she sits down on the edge of the bed and crosses her legs. "Hey, honey."

I put down the book with a sigh. "Hey, Mom."

"Honey, I'm supposed to go to Moravský Krumlov tomorrow to see the Slav Epic."

The Slav Epic is a series of twenty or so huge canvases that Mucha painted to tell the history of the Slavic peoples. The Communists are not big on Mucha, who they think of as a bourgeois sellout, and the canvases are kept in some ramshackle huge old manor house in a little Moravian village.

"Okay," I say.

"Fulbright set this up for me, and they've made special arrangements for me to meet with some scholars while I'm there, so it's not the kind of thing I want to reschedule, although I will if I have to."

"Go," I say, reaching for my book. "I'll be fine."

"Actually, I was wondering if you wanted to come with me," she says.

"Good one," I say. "Ha-ha."

"Hear me out. If you don't want to, you don't have to. Mrs. Svobodová said she can keep an eye on you, but she also pointed out that the Moravský Krumlov is only about twenty-five miles from Bavory, and she suggested we might like to go and spend the night with her sister-in-law."

"Anežka?" Merry says, looking up from her homework. "Oh, Mom, you've got to meet her. You'd love her."

"I'd like to," Mom says. "And it would be nice to have a

place to spend the night to break up the trip. But if you don't want to come, I can easily drive back tomorrow night ..."

"No," I say, feeling more energetic than I have in weeks. "No. I want to go."

"Can I come?" Merry asks.

I laugh evilly. "Tough banana peels, big sister. *You* can't miss any schooo-ooel."

"Another time, Merry," Mom says. She turns to me. "Just so you know, the appointment's for ten a.m. I won't have time to drop you in Bavory first, so you'll have to come with me to the manor house or whatever, but you can bring a book or something and as soon as I'm done we'll zip down in plenty of time for supper and a nice long visit before bed. Then we'll drive back Friday morning."

"Let me guess," Merry says. "I'm the one stuck with bringing Cory home from school, making dinner, putting her to bed, and getting her to school again."

"Cinderelly, Cinderelly, night and day it's Cinderelly," I warble. "Wash the dishes, do the mopping, and the sweeping and the dusting ..."

"Okay, okay, I'll do it."

"... they always keep her hopping. She goes around in circles till she's very, very dizzy—"

"Shut up, Jude! I mean it! Stop singing and I'll do it."

We leave at six-thirty so we'll be sure of getting there on time. Mom lets me make a nest in the back seat with pillows and blankets. I stick my feet up against the cold window, glad that I am wearing thick wool socks, and settle back with my Walkman. It feels like a holiday to be heading out of the city while everyone else is going to school and work, not to mention being in the back seat of the Volvo all by myself. I snuggle in against my down quilt, adjust the headphones more comfortably, and watch the brightening sky outside the car window as the car carries me toward Anežka. I remember that poem Merry likes so much:

The year's at the spring,
And day's at the morn;
Morning's at seven;
The hill-side's dew-pearl'd;
The lark's on the wing;
The snail's on the thorn;
God's in His heaven—
All's right with the world!

"Quote!" I want to say to Merry. But she's at school.

Holiday or not, it's a long, bumpy trip, and I'm glad when it ends. I climb out of the car, raining pretzel crumbs and apple cores onto the ground, and stretch. The air still tastes of coal, but much more faintly than in Prague, and here in the country it's overlaid with the clean, sharp scent of pine trees and rotting leaves.

We are parked next to a crumbling stucco wall on a country road that reminds me of jogging with Cory last summer in Meadowbrook. The road unrolls invitingly before me in the flat pearl light of the November day, and I think about going for a walk. Then a gust of bitter winter wind blasts around the corner and I change my mind. I follow Mom, who is waiting only semi-patiently, through the gates of the manor.

The house, which is set in a typically overgrown Czech garden, has that shabby, peeling-paint look that tells you that the inside is going to be drafty and uncomfortable. There's a little flock of clucking professors or curators or whatever they are, waiting inside the entrance. They shake our hands, they bid us welcome, they offer us coffee and mineral water and little dusty cakes, all the while telegraphing unmistakably that I have absolutely NO BUSINESS tagging along with the grownups. Fine with me. When everyone else puts on huge, open-back felt slippers that are supposed to save the wooden floor—which is dry and splintery and looks like it is far past a time when anyone would actually want to save it—and trudges upstairs to the beginning of the exhibition, I stay right where I am in a little office-y room and open a book.

It's a good one, but I've already been in veg mode for almost four hours, and after a chapter or two I get restless. I put it down and get up to find a bathroom.

When I'm done, I can hear everyone creaking around upstairs. Tired of sitting, I slip on a pair of gigantic felt slippers and skate up the stairs to see what there is to see.

The paintings are not at all what I expect after seeing other work by Mucha in books of Mom's—hard, intricate, poster-like Art Nouveau things of beautiful women with flowers in their swirly hair. These paintings are much softer than that, painted in matte, muted colors.

Despite their quiet colors, they are not quiet paintings. They are awesome—some must be twenty feet high and more than twenty-five feet wide. Slavs of all descriptions swarm across the paintings—men, women, children, pagans, Christians, farmers, scholars, princes, Russians, and Poles; preached to by missionaries, freed by tsars, and exhorted by saints. I'm not usually a museum kind of girl, but there's something about these paintings that pulls me right in. Then I turn a corner and stop dead.

Two figures in white stare at me, terrified. A man and his wife crouch in nighttime bushes while Goths burn their homes and fields. Their headdresses are crooked and they have the dead faces of those without hope.

They're me. They're me in the mirror at the hospital.

I don't want to look anymore. I go to find my book.

I stare at my book, but those faces get in the way. They're inside me. They are always waiting. They're in me, in my bones and cells and brain, and they will never go away.

I can't stay here anymore. I scribble a note to Mom, telling her to take all the time she needs with her experts but that I have gone to find Anežka. I grab my coat and my backpack and set off south for Mikulov.

It's cold at first, but I know I will warm up. The countryside is shriveled and frozen; I wish it were six weeks earlier, when the leaves were still on the trees. I think of how pleased Dr. Tanner will be when I tell him what happened. I am frightened, so I am choosing to do something about my feelings. I am going to find someone who can help me. And I'm doing it in a responsible way. I left a note for Mom and told her not to hurry. And instead of taking the car and driving to Vienna to try to find him, I have identified a reasonable substitute, Anežka, and am making arrangements to get what I need. It's only twenty-five miles or so. That's less than a marathon. And I'm walking, not running.

It's really pretty cold. My ears begin to ache and my nose is running, but I don't have anything to wipe it with. I'm getting hungry, too. I congratulate myself on remembering my backpack, which has some money in it for when I pass a restaurant or grocery store. And for going to the bathroom before I set off.

The tips of my fingers are numb and my eyes are tearing up from the cold. I wish I had a pair of gloves or mittens or something. And I wish I had Merry's glasses to protect my eyes from the wind. I imagine Merry right now, in some boring class worrying about whether she wrote the homework down right. I am so glad that I am where I am instead of where she is.

A car comes around the bend, traveling fast. I have time only to notice that it's blue and about four times bigger than most Czech cars before I see the brake lights go on and hear the tires squeal. As it backs quickly toward me, I realize that it's the good old Volvo.

"Hi, Mom," I say, opening the front passenger door. "If I'd known you'd be finished so quickly, I would have waited. Did they have interesting stuff to say?" I throw my backpack in the back and climb into the front seat next to her. "Gee, I'm starved. Do you think we'll be able to find a restaurant or café or something?"

"Judith Grace Wheelock, what the *hell* did you think you were doing?" she hisses at me. She is so angry that her hands are shaking on the wheel.

"Didn't you get my note?" I say, surprised.

"Of course I got your note," she says. "But you don't just waltz out of the exhibition and start wandering through Communist Moravia because you *feel* like it. What were you thinking?"

I feel my face go still. I hunch my shoulders and turn away as the car starts forward.

"They planned a luncheon. First I show up with an uninvited guest and then the guest goes wandering off. You know how paranoid these people are! I mean, come on, Jude, it's not brain surgery. Think things through, why don't you?"

We're still headed away from Moravský Krumlov. "Where are we going?" I ask. "I thought you had a fancy lunch."

"Well, you've ruined that," she says. Mom never talks to me and Merry and Cory this way. She must be really mad. "I'll drive you to Bavory and then come back for the afternoon session. Honestly, Jude. Where is your judgment?"

There's no answer to that.

We stop at a little *portaviny* halfway to Bavory and buy some bread, cheese, and small Czech apples. After we eat, Mom seems to relax a little bit and it occurs to me that she was probably really hungry and has already done a lot of driving today. I start thinking about how scary it must have been for her to find the little town and meet all the unfriendly Communist scholars and have to bring her daughter, and how she has probably been worried about me and having to drive to Nuremberg all the time, let alone how much the hospital must have cost. And now she's going to have to drive an extra hour and a half and mess up some big honorary luncheon and drop me at some lady's house that she doesn't even know and it might not be open.

I feel sick. I'm an idiot. How could I have been so stupid? The cheese turns to lead in my stomach and I feel the old familiar choking feeling, like I can't get enough air. I'm glad that I can't. I don't deserve to breathe. I'm bad and stupid and wicked. "I'm really sorry that I messed things up for you like that," I say to Mom, and start to cry. "I didn't mean to."

"I know, sweetheart," Mom says, sighing. "I know you're doing the best you can, and I'm doing the best I can, and sometimes the two don't line up just right. But we'll figure it out."

No one is home at Anežka's house, which looks bare and lonely in front of the leafless vines. But the door is unlocked, and I reassure Mom that Anežka won't mind a bit if I go in and wait for her there. I'm not sure Mom believes me, but she really doesn't have any choice, so she waves goodbye and drives off, looking at her watch.

The house is quiet except for the tick-tock of an old clock on the mantel in the living room. It smells of bread and dust, although it is very clean. I walk around, touching things. The heavy cotton brocade tablecloth on the table in the parlor. The cool porcelain shepherdess on the mantelpiece next to the clock. The smooth curve of the rocking chair's arm.

I trudge upstairs to the bed Anežka has made ready for me. She has put the books I was reading last time I was here on the end table, next to a vase of dried flowers and an oil lamp. All at once, I am very tired. I crawl in between the soft old cotton sheets.

THE **TREE** OF LIFE

I become aware of women's voices and the smell of meat cooking. It's dark and the room is cold, but my bed is soft and warm. I lie there drowsily for a few minutes, giving myself a chance to wake up.

Downstairs in the kitchen a chair scrapes; then I hear my mother's quick step crossing the living room and coming up the stairs. I sit up as the door creaks open.

"Hi, Mom."

"Hi, sleepyhead."

I squint at the dark windows. "What time is it, anyway?"

She perches on the bottom of my bed. "Almost six. You slept the day away."

"How did your seminar thing go?"

She rolls her eyes. "Fine. You made their day, running away like that. Lots of scope for meditations on the flightiness and lack of discipline of the bourgeois way of life."

"I'm really sorry, Mom."

She covers my hand with her own. "I know, hon. It's okay.

Like I said, it made their day and I got to see some pretty incredible paintings, so no harm's done. And I suppose it was unrealistic of me to think you could spend the day sitting there. It's just that I've waited so long to see these paintings …"

"No, it was my fault," I say.

"Well, it's over now," she says, getting to her feet. "I got to see the paintings, you got a nap you must have needed, and what smells like a wonderful dinner awaits. I like your Anežka."

Anežka is standing at the stove over a pan of boiling water. She puts down her spoon when she sees me and wipes her hands on her apron. "I am so sorry that I was not here to greet you," she says, stretching out her arms for a hug. "But I am glad that you made yourself comfortable in my absence. So, this has been an adventurous time for my little Judith, no?"

"Yeah, sort of," I say.

She brushes my hair back out of my face. "I must tell you that you are looking very much better than the last time I saw you. That was not a good evening. Well, we will eat and you will tell me about it. *Tak.* Your mama, she will sit here. You, there. So. Mrs. Virginia, do you wish to bless the food?"

"Yes, thanks," Mom says, surprised. "And, please, just Virginia."

She offers a brief prayer and we sit down to bratwurst, sauerkraut, rye bread, mustard, and stewed apples.

"*Dobrou chut'*," Anežka says.

"*Dobrou chut'*," we say. I am hungry, and the hot food tastes wonderful.

I roll the hot, spicy meat around in my mouth. Then the sweet apples. "This is ambrosia," I say. "The food of the gods."

"Judith, you have no idea how pleased I am to have you and your dear mother in my home," Anežka says.

"Anežka," Mom says thoughtfully. "Were you named after the saint?"

Anežka does not look up from spreading mustard on her bread. "Yes, that is so," she says.

"What saint?" I ask.

"Agnes of Bohemia," Mom says. "She was made a saint last Sunday."

"Who?"

Anežka puts down her bread and unfastens something that she is wearing around her neck. She hands it to me and I see that it is a small gold medal with a picture of a tree on one side and a saint on the other. "Anežka—or Agnes, as you say—was the youngest daughter of a thirteen-century Bohemian king," Anežka explains. "She was engaged to be married to the Holy Roman Emperor, but ran away and established a Franciscan abbey instead. There is an old prophecy that when Anežka becomes a saint, peace and happiness will come to the Czech lands. And last Sunday, Pope John Paul II declared her a saint. So now we wait for the peace and the happiness."

I'm surprised at the hint of bitterness in her voice. I don't know what to say, so I make a big deal of examining the medal. "And you were named after her?"

"Yes. I was born on her feast day, March second. My

grandfather was a jeweler, and he made that for my eighth birthday."

"Your *grandfather* made this?" I'm impressed. It is a beautiful thing, graceful and delicate. I pass it to Mom so that she can admire it.

"He must have been a very fine jeweler," Mom says.

"I think he was," Anežka says, "although I did not know him well. My mother was estranged from her parents until shortly before their deaths."

"I'm sorry to hear that," Mom says.

Anežka makes a brushing motion. "It is a long time ago. And a familiar story. She was their only daughter. Beautiful, well educated, talented. She was a medical student, but there was a flu epidemic and she became seriously ill. Her parents sent her to the country for a few weeks to recuperate. She stayed with one of her friends from boarding school. They lived in the castle we saw that day in Mikulov, Judith.

"One day she went for a walk and sprained her ankle," Anežka continues. "A young man in a cart happened by and rescued her. My father. He was a poor farmer, but they fell in love. Her parents objected, but she ran away and married him anyway. And, against every expectation, they lived happily ever after."

I take a long, satisfied breath. "A real-life fairy tale," I say.

"That is exactly what my mother always used to say," Anežka says. She stands up and starts to clear the plates. Mom and I try to help her but she won't let us. "No. You are my guests. Besides, the kitchen is only big enough for one."

We sit down again. "So that must be where all the furniture comes from," I say. "Your grandparents."

Anežka looks amused. "You have a busy mind, Judith. You are right. The furnishings do not match the house. Yes, some of it came from my mother's people. The rest came from my husband's people."

"Anežka's husband was a soccer player," I tell Mom. "Did I tell you that?"

"I don't think so. But you *did* say that she was a wonderful soccer ref. Is that how you met?"

Anežka puts some water on to boil. "No. We met as students at the university in Brno. Dušan studied medicine, I literature."

She lifts the dumplings out of the pot and puts them on a folded dish towel to drain.

"It is ironic, really. Neither of us would have been there except for the Communists. My family was under suspicion because my grandparents had been wealthy. They lost their business and their apartment, of course, and came to live with my parents. It was quite crowded—my father's mother also lived with us, and as you can see, this house is not very spacious. But the Communists approved of me, because my father was a poor farmer and I was a good athlete. So they admitted me to the university."

She puts a kettle on to boil.

"No coffee for me," Mom says as Anežka reaches for a small tin.

Anežka stops in mid-gesture and turns to us. "Not coffee," she says. "I had thought perhaps some herb tea?"

"Herb tea?" Mom says.

"From the linden tree," Anežka says. "It is a delicate tea, good for the digestion."

"That would be lovely," Mom says. "Jude? How about you?"

"Sure," I say. "So you weren't planning on going to college?"

Anežka laughs as she spoons dried flowers into a china pot and then adds the boiling water. "College? Me? I was a poor farmer's daughter. Going to college was something my mother might have done, but certainly not me. I took after my father's mother, a good, strong peasant woman who could wring a goose's neck without thinking twice. But I was no scholar. No one my age was. First the Depression, then the German occupation. I was lucky I could write my name."

She goes into the living room and returns, carrying three teacups and saucers on a small tray and a picture, which she hands to Mom. "My father's mother," she says. "Marketa."

Mom and I look at the faded photograph. A sturdy peasant woman in traditional dress stares back at us, obviously shy about having her picture taken. She holds curiously shapeless hands stiffly over her stomach. Her resemblance to Anežka is very strong.

"What is wrong with her hands?" I ask.

"She was a goose girl," Anežka says, as if that explains everything.

"What does that have to do with her hands?"

"She minded the village's geese as a girl. They would peck her hands when she fed them."

"How awful!" Mom says.

"It is hard work to be a peasant," Anežka says. She sets out delicate china plates, spoons, the teapot, and a small pot of honey.

"What about your husband's people?" Mom asks.

"They were quite well-to-do. His father was a physician in Brno. This would have been enough to keep Dušan out of university once the Communists came to power, except that a Russian flier had been shot down near their home a few weeks before the end of the war. Dušan's father had taken him into their home and tried to treat him secretly. But they were betrayed by a neighbor. The Germans raided their home, shot the Russian soldier and Dušan's parents, and sent Dušan and his younger brother to the camps. When the camps were liberated a few weeks later, Dušan and his brother were both Communist heroes."

She busies herself for another minute at the counter, arranging the dumplings on a china platter and sprinkling them with soft cheese and powdered sugar. Then she sets the platter on the table, removes her apron, and sits down heavily. "These are cherry dumplings," she says. "A Czech specialty. It is my grandmother's recipe."

They are so good that we stop talking so we can concentrate on our food.

"No," Mom says finally, when Anežka offers her another. "I couldn't possibly. I haven't eaten like this in months." She picks up the medal again, examining the graceful tree. "I've always loved the smell of linden blossoms, of course, but I didn't know it was such a useful tree. A real tree of life."

Anežka's face freezes. She starts to say something, then stops. She gives Mom a tight little smile and then drops her hands into her lap and stares at them, her back very straight.

"Did I say something wrong?" Mom asks in her Relief Society voice, that kind, wise, loving voice that makes you want to tell her everything.

"No, no, of course not. I just have not heard that phrase for a long ... That was what my mother used to ..." Her voice breaks and she covers her eyes with her hands.

Mom and I look at each other.

Anežka pulls a tissue from beneath the sleeve of her sweater and begins to dab at her eyes. "I'm terribly sorry, Virginia, Judith. Excuse me, please. I do not know what has come over me." She tries to smile at us and cannot. She reaches for the plates and begins to get up.

Very gently, Mom reaches across the table and lays her hand on Anežka's. "Would you like to talk about it?" she says. "Because if you would, we would like to hear."

Anežka looks down at Mom's hand on her arm and hesitates. After a moment, she lets go of the dishes and sinks back into her seat. She covers Mom's smooth, manicured hand with both of her big, gnarled ones and pats it. "You have a good heart, Virginia, but I do not know if the little one—"

"It's okay," I say. "Really. I'd like to hear your story."

So she tells us.

Anežka met her husband shortly after she arrived at the university. Brno had been struck by a week of torrential rains, capped by a night of unusually high winds. On her way to school the next morning, Anežka had ridden past a small linden tree uprooted by the storm. A boy about her age sat next to it in a bathrobe and pajamas, sobbing with his head in his hands. Dušan's younger brother, Tomáš.

"He'd been home from the camps for almost a year by then, but he still had the look," she says, gazing into space as she warms her hands on her teacup. "Eyes like bruises, and skin so thin and pale you half expected his bones to tear through it." She blinks and looks at us. "You are too young to remember, but there were some who saw things during the war that ... changed them.

"Foolish girl that I was, I asked him if he was all right. Of course he said he was fine, he was just upset because his parents, who were dead, had planted the tree for him when he was born. 'If it's that important to you, why don't you plant it again?' I asked. His older brother had told him it couldn't be saved. I told him that his brother didn't know what he was talking about, that I had been raised on a farm and that we had saved trees bigger than that one many times and that as long as the root ball was more or less intact and still moist, it was worth a try. So we got it back up and staked it, and just as we finished here comes big brother Dušan. I straighten up, ready to be congratulated for my selflessness—my dress was completely ruined and we had worked right through all my classes—but instead, this young man whom I have never met grabs me by the arm, drags me around the corner out of earshot, and proceeds to give me the biggest scolding of my life. What the devil did I think I was doing? Anyone with half a brain could tell that Tomáš had been through a lot, and the last thing he needed was to have his heart broken one more time by some ineffectual do-gooder who had nothing better to do than wandering around the city making promises she couldn't keep."

The tree recovered, although Tomáš never did. He joined a monastery a few months later, about the time Anežka and Dušan were married. By the beginning of 1950, Dušan was studying medicine and Anežka had decided to become a professor of literature.

"That is when I discovered I was pregnant," Anežka tells us. "We were overjoyed. In those days you weren't supposed to give monks gifts, so we decided to save the news for Tomáš's birthday at the end of April. I was just beginning to show, and I made my first maternity dress, red with yellow stripes, especially for the visit."

The Communist government did not approve of religion, however, or of monks who wasted their time on prayer when they could be working to strengthen the state. In the middle of the night on Thursday, April 13, government troops stormed all of Czechoslovakia's monasteries and sent the monks to concentration camps.

"Dušan was frantic," Anežka says, tracing the pattern of the lace tablecloth with the tip of her spoon. "He knew poor Tomáš would not survive a second incarceration. He did everything he could to find his brother. But he was unsuccessful, and in searching he had drawn attention to himself, which was a dangerous thing to do."

One night a few weeks later, the young couple awoke to a gang of thugs trashing their apartment. When the thugs had finished with the apartment, they started on Dušan and Anežka, beating them until they were near death.

"I lost the baby, of course," Anežka says. She is quiet for a moment, her hands going to the emptiness in her stomach. "Do you know what was hardest? I never knew if it was a boy or a girl. I had carried this little being in my body for all those months, and I never knew what it was. Then, afterwards, I could not have any more."

Her husband, who had been training to be a surgeon, lost an eye and the use of his left leg. The government assigned him to be a cashier at the hospital's cafeteria to remind his colleagues what happened to people who asked questions.

"Nothing happened to me," Anežka says. "After the beating, I mean. We kept expecting it to, but it never did. I graduated without any problem and became a teacher. Perhaps they thought that my success would make things harder for my husband. I do not know. But it didn't. He was always very proud of me."

When the thaw came in 1968, Anežka was offered a visiting professorship in Canada. "We thought it would be a new start," she says. "I resigned my post at the university at the end of July and we went home to Bavory for a few weeks before the fall term started in Ottawa. My parents were dead, you see, and my grandmother was getting quite frail, so the plan was that we would pack up the farm and help move her to my brother's apartment in Prague. But we waited a little too long."

The grandmother of the misshapen hands died three days after the first Russian tanks rolled into Czechoslovakia.

Shortly after that, Anežka received word that her exit visa had been canceled. Two weeks later, Dušan went out to milk the cows. Anežka was taking a shower when she heard something that sounded like shots. She threw on clothes and got outside in time to see an unmarked van disappearing over the hill. She ran into the barn, only to discover a dead cow, an overturned milking stool, and a trail of blood. The border patrol found Dušan's body in the field we had seen that day from the castle in Mikulov. He had been shot more than one hundred times.

"The official story was that they caught him trying to cross the border and he resisted arrest, but everyone knew it was because we were leaving."

"Did you go back to Brno?" Mom asks.

Anežka purses her lips and shakes her head. "No, no. Such a thing would never have been allowed after I had tried to emigrate. They made me the groundskeeper at the castle in Mikulov."

I imagine Anežka working through the seasons in the gardens with the perfect view of the meadow where her husband's body had lain, and then I think of Tomáš lying in his monastic cell, listening as the barbarians came for him for the second time and praying for deliverance that never arrived.

"After a few years, I was reassigned as an assistant teacher at the nursery school," Anežka says.

"That must have been a blessing," Mom says.

"Indeed it was," Anežka says.

Mom arranges her teaspoon so that it is perfectly aligned with her empty teacup. "What a noble life you have lived,

Anežka," she says. "You make me quite ashamed of my small troubles."

"Tsk, tsk," Anežka scoffs. "I have survived, that is all. Survival is not noble. It is necessary."

"Just because something has to be done doesn't mean that it isn't noble," I say, too loudly because it is hard to get words past the pictures.

Anežka gives me an affectionate look. "Thank you, my Judith. That is a very gracious thing for you to say. But I must say that I was never tempted by survival's alternative. I'm much too fond of my food, for one thing. It is my peasant blood, perhaps." She pats her broad tummy and smiles at me.

She wants me to laugh. To *laugh*, after the story she has told us. I am consumed by rage that is hot and inexorable as a lava flow. "It's not a joke," I say. "You have no *right*, no right at all, to pretend—"

"Judith Grace!" Mom gasps.

"—that things are okay. That any of the things you told us can be made right. They can't. They are horrible and tragic. They're ... they're an obscenity. I don't even have the words to ... to express—" I am crying, deep burning sobs that bring no relief. "Where did it go? What did you do with it?"

"Do with what, my Judith?" Anežka asks gently.

"They hurt you," I try to explain. I mop at my eyes and nose, but they just get wet again. "They took everything away. It's *not* all right. *None* of it is right."

"Are you asking me what I did with my anger? How I made sense of all this?"

"Anežka, there's no need—" my mother begins.

"No, no," Anežka says. "These are important questions. You are right to ask them, my Judith." She picks up her medal from where it lies on the tablecloth and gently brushes her thumb across the linden tree while she decides how to answer me.

"At least you're *here*," I say. "At least you survived. But what about Tomáš? And Dušan? Why didn't God take care of them? Why didn't He make it all right for *them*?"

"*Judith*," Mom says again.

Anežka ignores her, still concentrating on the medal. "You are asking two things," she says at last. "First, what did I do to heal myself of anger and bitterness so that I could once again believe life was good? And second, how could I possibly be so selfish as to believe that life was good after Tomáš and Dušan—and our baby—were sacrificed?"

I start to say something, but she doesn't let me. "Don't worry, my Judith. I know you would never ask it in those words, but that is the gist, yes? I will answer the second question first, if I may. It is that I decided I could not presume to judge whether the lives of Tomáš and Dušan were tragic or not. I know they *ended* tragically. But it is perhaps possible to believe that your life has value and purpose no matter how it ends. No wife could have loved her husband more than I loved my Dušan, but I cannot tell you if his life was meaningful or not. It was meaningful to *me*. This I know. But to him? That I cannot say. I believe so, yes. But I do not know. Finally I do not think it is my responsibility to know. In the end, the only person who can make sense of a life is the person who lives it."

That is not what I want her to say.

She sees this on my face. "Ah, my poor Judith," she says, laughing a little. "Some small part of you still wishes for the fairy tale, is that it? Where good is good and bad is bad and every hard question has an answer. I will tell you this, although you will not believe me. It would not take you long to become tired of such a life."

Her smile fades. "As to the other—what I did with my anger ..." She hesitates. "Since you ask, I will tell you, although this, also, may be too personal a journey to be useful to another. It was easier at first, because Dušan was there, and he needed me." She glances at Mom. "I do not know if you agree, Virginia, but I find that it is very much easier to do difficult things for those you love than it is to do them for yourself."

Mom nods her agreement.

"When he ... died, it became much more difficult. There was no one to see if I grieved or behaved badly, so I indulged myself. In fact, I wallowed. Then one day I woke up and remembered that it was my grandmother's birthday. I went to the beer garden after work to have a slivovitz in her honor. I remember lifting the glass up to heaven, and then drinking. It was night, you know, and the lights were on, and I caught a glimpse of my reflection in the window. I looked terrible, just awful, sad and bitter and a little bit drunk, and all at once I remembered something my grandmother used to say to me. 'Choose carefully, because everything you do invites the world to live or die.'"

She smiles briefly at us. "That one glimpse had been enough

to tell me that at the moment, I was most certainly inviting the world to die." She looks off into space. "I went home and lay awake on my bed and decided that it was time for me to make a choice one way or the other. Either the world made sense or it did not. So I started a list. Such a man as Dušan had been born, and I had not only known him but been his wife. This suggested that the world was a good place, that it made sense. But men without understanding or virtue had been allowed to destroy him. The world did not make sense. Back and forth, back and forth, all night long. Finally, near morning, I realized that there were many arguments that could be made on both sides, and that in the end I would have to choose without knowing. I lay there and thought, I cannot do this alone. It matters too much, and I am too sad and weak to make a good decision. I had never felt so alone in my life, and I began to weep."

Anežka glances at us. "I should explain that as a child I suffered from terrible sinus infections. I would put my poor head on my mother's lap, and she would stroke my forehead and put cold compresses on it and recite poetry and Bible verses and anything she could think of to take my mind off the pain. Well, there I was, forty years later, lying on my bed, wretched and alone, and suddenly I felt my mother's cool hands stroking my forehead. She was saying something, too—it wasn't that I could hear the words, but they were there, in my mind, as clearly as if she had spoken. It was one of her Bible verses. I don't know how you would say it in English—something about hope delayed, hope prevented ..."

"Hope deferred," Mom says quietly.

"You know it?" Anežka says.

Mom nods. *"Hope deferred maketh the heart sick; but when the desire cometh, it is a tree of life,"* Mom quotes. "It's in Proverbs."

"That is the one," Anežka says. "I had heard her say it a hundred times, and remembered it hundreds more, but I suddenly realized that I had never really understood what it meant. I had always thought that when it said that the desire came—how is it, Virginia?"

"When the desire cometh, it is a tree of life," Mom repeats.

"I had always interpreted that line to mean 'When your desire is accomplished, then you will be happy.' Now I suddenly understood that that was not it at all—that the tree of life was planted by the desire itself. The thing that makes life rich and fruitful is not having what you want, but having a desire for something better—having something to work for and look forward to."

She shakes her head. "It was such a small change to make: thinking of what I could do to make things better instead of asking myself over and over why I and my family must suffer. And I do not mean to suggest that things changed overnight. But gradually I found that I had no room for the anger and bitterness, and they began to drop away."

She makes it sound so simple. "It's as easy as that, is it?" I say. "Just say no to ugliness, and the world magically transforms itself into a good place?"

I am behaving badly and I know it, but Anežka is unperturbed. "What you describe is denial," she says. "Not hope. Hope may be many things, but it is rarely easy—something that I think you may understand better than most, my Judith."

She pushes her chair back from the table and stands up slowly, as though her body hurts her. "Now I must thank you for listening to the ramblings of an old woman who has spent too many hours by herself." She brushes her big, crooked hand against my mother's cheek. "This evening has been a gift I will not forget," she says.

She turns to me, holding out a hand. Automatically I stretch out my hand in return. A second later, when the cold weight of the medal slips into my palm, I wish I hadn't. "I hope you will accept this as a small token of an evening that has been very precious to me, my Judith. Wear it in good health."

I fumble for an appropriate response, but she does not seem to expect one.

"And so," she adds briskly, "to bed."

APART

I lie next to my mother in the darkness, listening to her breathe. In, out. In, out. It is almost as though Merry is here with me. Almost, but not quite. My mother kept me safe when she was awake, but now that she is asleep, my strength seeps away and the nightmares come.

Far across a dark field, the white Slavs—who I know now are Anežka and her Dušan—wait for a miracle that will not come. The barbarians are coming, the ground shakes with their horses' hoofbeats, and Anežka begs Dušan to leave her, to run to safety, but he will not.

Now the barbarians are upon them. I strain to see what is happening, but the horses are too thick on the ground. Suddenly a pale hand stretches out from the melee and a thin gold disc is spinning toward me through the night. The universe slows, adjusts itself, and clicks into place. This is the moment I was born for. I reach up and pluck Anežka's medal from the thick night air.

As my fingers touch its cold, smooth surface, the noise and

fury of the battle falls from the air. It is the miracle! I spin around, jubilant, holding my prize high in triumph.

But there is no one to see. The trampled field is empty—empty except for Anežka cradling Dušan's broken body, a body that even as I watch begins to sink into the unforgiving mud.

The field begins to shake again. The barbarians are coming back. And this time, they are coming for me.

I wake, shaking and sick.

When the sky is finally light, I get up and wash. I put on my clothes. I help Mom make the bed; then we go downstairs to breakfast and hug Anežka goodbye.

I climb into the back seat, into my little nest, but I cannot sleep. Anežka's medal is too heavy. It chokes me. When we get home, I unfasten it from my neck and push it to the back of a drawer in my desk, but that makes no difference. I can still feel its cold weight against my throat.

I climb into my bed and pull the sheets over my head. I know that if I try to stand, the weight of the medal will strangle me.

I must have fallen asleep, because the sun is pouring in the window. But that's not right! We are supposed to be gone by now. I sit up in bed, my heart pounding, and check the time. It's after eleven o'clock. Why am I here? I should be in Germany.

I start to throw the covers back, but the room swings around me. "Mom!" I call, so frightened that something has gone badly wrong that at first I am afraid that my throat has forgotten how to speak. "Mom!"

I hear her quick footsteps in the hall and it is enough to take the edge off my dread. I sink back against my pillows as she pushes open my bedroom door, carrying a tray with some muffins, a glass of milk, and my meds. "Why are we still here?" I demand. "What about my appointment?"

"There was some trouble last night," Mom says, making room for the tray on my desk and handing me my meds and the milk. I swallow obediently. "A demonstration that got out of hand. There are rumors that a student was killed, and with all the upheaval in Germany the American Embassy asked us to stay put as a precaution. Your father called Dr. Tanner this morning, and he has scheduled a telephone session with you instead."

She hands me a raisin bran muffin cut in half that she has spread with cream cheese. I feel her watching me.

"It's nothing to worry about, sweetheart. I'm sure things will be back to normal in no time."

Normal.

I force myself to take a bite of the muffin, but it tastes like sawdust. I barely have the energy to push it away and pull the covers up over my head.

"Sweetheart," Mom says, sounding worried. "You didn't eat anything at all yesterday."

"I'm not hungry," I tell the cool white sheet.

"But Dr. Tanner said that it was important to have food with the meds."

"Maybe later," I say.

I love the blankness of the sheet draped over my face. There are no edges here. No stopping places. I remember the blue balls from physics class that could carry everything without stopping. That is what I have always wanted. To be carried on and on, to never stop. It's the stopping that is dangerous. If you stop, you might put down roots, and when it is time to go you will tear things and break them, even though you do not want to, even when you would give everything you have to feed them and water them and take care of them, but how can you? Because your brain is wrong, and there is a creature in you. You will always make mistakes, always. And sometimes those mistakes will hurt other people besides you.

So I lie there, loving my white sheet and feeling my edges disappear until I am gone, I am apart, and I cannot hurt anyone ever again. Voices talk to me, but I know that they belong to the creatures. They are trying to trick me, to lure me back so that they can use me to hurt and break things, to disappoint Lexy and scare Cory and break my parents' hearts.

It is dark, and then it is light. They try to feed me, but I don't want to help the creatures inside of me, so I turn away. It is getting dark again, and now the dread is returning. Dr. Tanner said they are just feelings. But they are stronger than I am. I cannot bear it. I will not bear it. But my mind is too shattered to plan.

There is a new voice. A Czech voice. But the creatures do not speak Czech. It belongs to a man in a shabby suit. He is from the StB, come to take Anežka's hope.

"I won't tell you where it is," I tell him, my throat rusty.

"It's all right, Jude," Dad says. "He is here to give you a blessing."

I look again, and he is the bishop whose neighbors watch him from behind their lace curtains.

"You shouldn't be here!" I say, furious. "They will see you!" Don't they understand I am trying to keep them safe?

The bishop says something, but I do not listen. I am afraid of what the creatures might do.

"Don't you understand? You've got to go! Dad, tell him. He's got to go. They'll know he's with us."

"I think the bishop probably understands that much better than we do, honey," Dad says.

I try to get up to push him away, but the room swings around me. I begin to cry, huge, wracking sobs. "Why won't anyone listen to me?" I cry. "He can't be here. Tell him he has to go."

The bishop comes closer, and I grab at his heavy worker's hands, desperate to make him understand. "You have to go," I plead. "Please. You must go."

He shakes his head, making shushing noises until I am still. "Judith," he says in a thick accent. "Listen to me. I am here for Jesus Christ. He cannot be here with you, so He has sent me."

I look at the bishop's tired, stony eyes, at his whiskery face and the shabby tie he has knotted so carefully. He looks like his countrymen, anonymous, poor, hoping not to be noticed. *There is no beauty that we should desire him.* No beauty. Just a bruised, stooped creature who lives a sad, imperfect life in a sad, imperfect place.

I'm not worth what this will do to you, I want to tell him. *I am a stupid American teenager. Save this for your own people.*

A picture appears in my mind. A picture of Brother

Ehrlich, bearing his testimony a few hours after his wife's death. Telling us we were his family. That he and his wife had thought of us as their children. That they had loved us.

He is here, a voice that is not mine tells me, *to be used*. Someone else was ordinary. Someone else was there to be used. But I am too tired to remember who. I close my eyes and turn away. I cannot do what must be done. I am broken. I am not worthy. *Just let me go*, I pray. *Here is Your breath. I give it to You freely. But please, let this end. I cannot be what You need me to be. Let me go.*

I open my eyes. Cory is watching me from outside my bedroom door. She is not supposed to be here. She is supposed to leave me alone. But she is here, watching me. Watching to see what I will do. Waiting for me to show her the way things are.

I close my eyes, then open them again. But she is still there.

Cory gave me her piece of the Wall.

I have nothing to give her. Only Anežka's medal, and that is not safe. Anežka, who has been alone so long that her heart is sick. I don't want Cory's heart to be sick. *Go away!* I think at her. *Go away! I cannot do this for you.*

But her eyes are still watching.

They took her closet. They took her room.

She needs me to stay. But how can I, when I will fail her over and over again?

From nowhere, a memory brushes against me, sweet as the smell of a linden flower. Me, flying, with a child in my arms. A child whom I understood. A child who understood me. A child whom I loved. A child who loved me. A child who made me true.

Together, we are enough, the Child tells me. *We will always be enough.*

Slowly, painfully, I discover what I must do. I struggle up, through my despair and shame, until I am sitting. I wait for a moment, willing the trembling to stop, but it doesn't. "Can we do it in here?" I whisper to Dad.

"Right here, sweetheart," he says.

Dad sits behind me and I lean against him. The bishop stands next to us both, and they put their hands on my head. The bishop pours a little oil on my hair and anoints me in Czech. Then Dad begins to talk, and because the Child is with me, making me true, I can let his words in.

"Judith Grace Wheelock," my father says. "In the name of Jesus Christ, I have the privilege of giving you a father's blessing, to heal and to comfort you in an hour of need. Judith, your Heavenly Father is mindful of the wounds that you bear. He reminds you that these companions, while the source of pain and confusion, are not badges of shame, but rather the means to direct you to a greater knowledge of your Heavenly Father's love for you, greater knowledge of His Son, and greater peace and power as they awaken you to new possibilities and ideas. He reminds you that His own beloved Son, after His resurrection, chose to retain the wounds He bore for His people in His perfected body; that these wounds, indeed, became the mark by which His people know Him. This is the great promise of the gospel—that every wound patiently borne will not only be healed, but will become the agent of great joy."

We are all crying when it is done—except for the bishop. He pats my shoulder once. "Is better?" he asks.

"Much better," I say, mopping at my drippy face. "Thank you for coming." I am embarrassed by how small the words are, but I have no others.

He clicks his heels and bows. As he is a small, shabby man, the gesture should seem absurd, but it does not. "I am happy to be used."

"Bishop, we are so deeply grateful ..." Mom begins, then can't finish. She pulls herself together. "May we at least offer you some refreshment?"

"I think the bishop is probably eager to be on his way," Dad says.

The bishop looks at the ceiling and considers. "Thank you, dear lady," he says. "That would be most pleasant."

"Are you sure?" Dad asks, looking concerned. "I mean ..."

It takes the bishop a moment to gather his words. "*For God hath not given us the spirit of fear; but of power, and of love, and of a sound mind*," he quotes. Then, unbelievably, he winks at us. "Besides, it may be that our curious friends are much occupied elsewhere."

That night, when the dream returns, I am ready. I pull the gold medal from the air, and the noise stops. I turn to Anežka and her Dušan, determined this time to stand as a witness so they will not have to bear their sorrow alone. Once again, she cradles his broken body. Once again, it begins to fall from her grasp. Once again, the field begins to tremble.

But this time I see that it is not trembling because of the return of the barbarian host. It is trembling because Dušan's broken body is taking root. It begins to grow, tendrils unfolding like a garden in bloom, until soon he has grown into a linden tree, which is the tree of life. His branches lean over Anežka, protecting her, and his trunk glows in the night, showing the way.

As soon as it realizes that I am awake, fear comes licking at my edges, blurring them so that I don't know where I end and the world begins. *They're just feelings,* I tell myself. But they are feelings that come back and back and back. They will always be there, waiting.

I don't want to be here. I want to be with Anežka while the tree that is Dušan keeps us safe. I turn in to my nest, pushing the day away.

But the click pulls me back, the little click that says that it's 6:30 on a school day and time to get up. Static crackles as the clock radio switches on to Radio Free Europe, and here's John Denver, singing about Poems and Prayers and Promises behind the static of the Communists trying to jam the station.

"Turn it *off,*" Merry moans. Her hand pats around the nightstand, trying to find the snooze button.

She finally gets it, and the singing stops. She lies there for a minute, recovering, then manages to prop herself up against the pillows. "Count on good old John Denver to hunt us down wherever we are," she moans. "Will we never escape?" Merry *despises* John Denver.

Then she says something about hoping Dad didn't hear

it, because the stupid songs stick in your stupid head, and now Dad will probably sing stupid John Denver songs on the stupid bus all the way to the stupid school …

"Earth to Jude," Merry says loudly.

"What?"

"So are you going to school today, or what?"

I throw back my covers. "Yeah," I say. "Think I will."

"Good," she says, and heads for the bathroom.

I start to dress, but stop when I am zipping up my pants. I go to my desk and rummage around until I find Lexy's address. I steal an aerogram from the pile on Merry's desk, write the address on it, and fold it up and put it away in my back pocket so I won't forget.

There's a little knock on the door while I am putting on my socks. "Yeah?" I say.

Cory opens the door but doesn't come in. "Mom wanted me to find out if you were up to school today," she says.

"Yep," I say.

She turns to go.

"Hey, Cory," I say. "You doing anything special after school?"

She shakes her head.

"You want to take our blades to Letná Park and slap a puck around?"

Her face lights up. "You bet," she says.

No one believes the strike will work. No one.

But we are wrong.

The first night, while I fire pucks at Cory so that she won't think about the demonstration, Good King Wenceslas watches fifty thousand of his people gather before him. They are poorly dressed and shiver in the bitter cold, but they pull their keys from their pockets and shake them until they ring like bells, and hold their cigarette lighters up like candles. The next night, there are a hundred thousand. By Saturday, there are half a million, so many that we gather at Letná Plain. We look down at the city gleaming gold in the setting sun, like the warrior queen Libuše once did from her castle at Vyšehrad, and we sing and light candles against the winter darkness until word comes that the Communists have resigned.

On New Year's Day, 1990, we make our way to Prague Castle along with the rest of Czechoslovakia. We stand in the courtyard with the Svobodas and Anežka and Sunil's family and Lexy, who spent Christmas with her mother in Switzerland and is now spending New Year's with us in Prague. My Christmas present jumps on me and breathes her sweet, wet breath on my face—Toby, who waited patiently in quarantine—and we cannot stop laughing because no one guessed, six weeks before, not one person in the world could possibly have guessed that we would be celebrating the inauguration of Václav Havel as Czechoslovakia's democratically elected president.

In his speech, Havel promises that when we examine ourselves truthfully, unafraid of imperfection and responsibility, "hope will return to our hearts." He urges us to join him in "the art of the impossible," living lives that look forward to what may be, as well as backward to what has already been.

While he speaks, Anežka's hand goes to her throat and gently brushes *her* Christmas present, which is back where it belongs. And then we have to hurry home, because there are treats to set out for the Czech saints who are coming to our house to sing and sing and sing.

ACKNOWLEDGMENTS

The genesis of this novel was a Fulbright-Hays Seminar Abroad for educators in Slovakia and the Czech Republic during the summer of 2003. I am unutterably grateful to Anne Clift Boris, Marcela Grošeková, Nora Hlozeková, Katarina Kanabová, Kristina Pazitna, Hana Ripková, and Don Sparling for making that magnificent experience possible. I also owe substantial debts of gratitude to a variety of experts who generously took the time to share their knowledge of Czech culture, history, and current affairs including (but not limited to) Helena Ackerman, Tony Ackerman, Cleo Appleton, John Boris, Olga Campora, John Crane, Barbara Day, Jakub Dürr, Jakub Kyncl, Marie Neudorflová, Kezelka Ondrej, Pavel Ripka, Zdena Sparling, and Tomáš Vlček, as well as Dr. Robert O. Friedel, author of *Borderline Personality Demystified,* who unaccountably agreed to vet a manuscript whose assemblage of themes must have sounded odd even to his jaded ears.

I began this project during a term-long sabbatical granted by the Waterford School and ended it as I hope always to do: being saved from myself by Katya Rice, Front Street's gracious and eagle-eyed copy editor. The long journey in between was shorter than it might otherwise have been, thanks to the helpful comments of John Bennion, Nancy Heuston, Lynn Lonsdale, and Carol Lynch Williams. Sandra Camargo, Dusty Heuston, Linda Kitchen, and the folks at Johanna's Kitchen facilitated the book in ways that were no less valuable, if less obviously literary. Helen Robinson designed the beautiful cover.

In the years before her death, my sister Kary repeatedly urged me to consider writing a book with her. Demonstrating the good sense that is my trademark, I just as repeatedly declined. And yet, somehow, here it is. I don't know how it happened. But I know it wouldn't have without the patience and skill of my infuriatingly wonderful editor, Stephen Roxburgh. Thank you, Stephen, for giving Kary the last word one more time.